Emma Berry Mystery series

Saddled with Death
A Gem of a Problem
A Body in the Woodpile
Murder at the Mill
Death in Disguise

MURDER
at the
MILL

An Emma Berry Mystery
Book #4

Irene Sauman

Jakada Books

PERTH WESTERN AUSTRALIA

Murder at the Mill: Irene Sauman
Jakada Books / Perth Western Australia

Publisher's Note: This is a work of fiction. Names, characters, places, and incidents are a product of the author's imagination. Locales and public names are sometimes used for atmospheric purposes. Any resemblance to actual people, living or dead, or to businesses, companies, events, institutions, or locales is completely coincidental.

Cover art: Elements by Sheldon, ArtisanViking.

Paperback ISBN: 978-0-6454212-0-0

Dedication

This book is dedicated to
the memory of my grandmother
Alice Bennett
who started married life on a riverboat.

Author's Note

The Emma Berry mysteries are set in the 1870s on the Murray River, the third longest navigable river in the world, surpassed only by the Amazon and the Nile. Its great navigable length was responsible for the development of the riverboats, the sidewheel paddle steamers that opened up the Australian countryside along the river's length to settlement and sheep farming, in much the way railways did in the wider countryside.

Indeed, it was the railways that eventually ended the glory days of the paddle steamers, though they continue to ply the waters in the 21st century, carrying tourists and holiday makers. Two generations of my father's family produced working riverboat captains. But this story is strictly fiction.

Murder at the Mill is the fourth title in this series.

Main Characters

<u>At Wirramilla on the Murray</u>
Edward & Rose Haythorne: pastoralists
Emma Berry,: their widowed daughter
Eleanor Haythorne: Edward's mother
Lucy Wirra: housekeeper
Sal, Jacky & Janey Wirra: Lucy's adult children
Nella Brackett: Lucy's eldest married to overseer Jeff
  Brackett, children: Jack, Elly, Billy

<u>At Nettifield on the Murray</u>
George Macdonald: pastoralist, widower
His adult children: Matty, Beatrice (Bea), Jim
Thomas Quilp: overseer, Bea's betrothed

<u>The paddle steamer *Mary B*</u>
Daniel Berry: Captain, Emma's brother-in-law
Crew: Fred Croaker, Shorty Mason, Blue Higgins,
  Willy Bowman, Ah Lo (Charley)

<u>At River Bend on the Darling</u>
Mrs. Isabel Lockwood: widow
Her adult children: Andrew, Barbara, Declan, Evan,
  Frank, Harold, Ian
Ruth Lockwood: Andrew's wife
Naomi Lockwood: Declan's wife
Mrs. Fowler, housekeeper
Maids: Gladys, Holly, Maudie
Brendan O'Neill: odd-job man
Deelie O'Neill: his wife, children: Liam, Orla
Rory Felling: blacksmith, wife Janet
Ann Russell: schoolteacher
Jack Brighten: miller

<u>At Wentworth</u>

Joseph (Joe) Haythorne: Emma's brother, a
    Customs Officer
Catherine Haythorne: Joe's wife, infant Theodore
Tom Gulbis: livery stable owner, ex-convict, father
    of Ruth & Naomi Lockwood
Dotty Keogh: Keogh's Drapery Store
Lieutenant Forrester: police officer
Dr. Wilson, local medical man
Mrs. Wilson: his wife, daughter Zoe, niece Lizzie
    Ballard

<u>Fires in Ships and Mills</u>. To the Editor. Sir-I see that the... venturesome shareholders of the South Australian Insurance Company have a Christmas-box in the shape of another burnt flour-mill... It is time that mill-owners should learn how to put up fireproof buildings for such a dangerous trade; and the way to teach them the lesson, is to refuse to insure mills built on the present system. *Adelaide Observer,* Sat 1 January 1870

<u>Explosions in flour mills</u>. Doctor Stevenson Macadam has recently read to the Royal Scottish Society of Arts a paper upon this subject, and the following are the conclusions set forth in his paper. In the first place, he said, he came to the conclusion that a mixture of flour dust and air in certain proportions was explosive, and that when air and flour were exploded in confined spaces, a pressure equal to eight atmospheres was produced. *The Age,* Sat 8 March 1873, p. *7*

Chapter 1

A Visit with Catherine & Joe

Sunday 4 April 1876

"I DON'T KNOW what you can be thinking to go visiting with servants," Rose Haythorne grumbled, not for the first time. The morning room where they sat might be bright with the autumn sun, but no amount of pleasant weather seemed to lighten Rose's mood today.

Emma helped herself to a slice of Lucy's moist fruit cake and didn't comment. It was the easiest way of dealing with her mother's grumbles. Her grandmother had her nose in a book as she sipped her tea and took no notice. The book was her own latest Trollope, Emma saw: *The Way we Live Now*. Perhaps something her mother should read instead.

"If anyone asks where you are, I will have to tell them you are visiting Joseph and Catherine in Wentworth," Rose continued.

"The only person likely to ask is Daniel when he brings the *Mary B* downriver, and I will be visiting Joe and Catherine, Mother," Emma responded, thinking of her brother and sister-in-law and their new infant. "Anyway, the invitation to visit River Bend came from Mrs. Lockwood."

At Deelie O'Neill's request, but if Brendan's employer was happy enough to write the letter for the Irish girl Emma felt welcome to visit. She couldn't tell her mother that without the help of Deelie and Brendan six month ago she might never have found the emerald necklace Sam lost when the *Mary B* sank. Her mother knew nothing about that particular incident. Besides, she wasn't a stranger to Mrs. Lockwood either, having met her at the same time.

It had been restful back home at Wirramilla during the off-season, for the most part, but she would be glad to have the boards of the *Mary B* underfoot again. She wondered how Daniel had managed his time on his own. At least he'd had the *Mary B*'s Jack Russell for company while the boat had been moored in Rotten Row, downstream from the Echuca wharf.

The water levels in the Murray River and its tributaries had been high enough for a new season of trade for several weeks now, but Daniel had taken work up the Murrumbidgee and east to Albury and hadn't come as far west as Wirramilla. His last letter suggested he would be up in another couple of weeks. Time enough for her little holiday. She had another reason for spending time at Wentworth too, which her mother knew nothing about.

Emma's fox terrier Floss, asleep at her feet, snuffled and twitched. Emma bent down and patted her. Floss grunted and flipped an ear. The little dog shared her devotion between Emma and her grandmother these days, which meant Floss didn't miss Emma too much now when she was away and forgave her absences.

"Well, I suppose that is at least something," Rose said. "The Lockwoods have a successful property on the Darling River. There's a large family, I understand." She sniffed. "The boys run the place since their father died."

That would be a dig at Joe who wasn't interested in inheriting Wirramilla. He preferred his job with the Customs Office.

"Everyone has to make their own choices in life," Eleanor Haythorne said looking up, her green eyes a mirror image of Emma's own as she smiled at her granddaughter. "And friends are friends no matter their station."

Lucy Wirra came in and began to clear the morning tea things, loading the teacups and plates onto a tray, her brown hands nimble and sure. Emma picked up the teapot and followed Lucy to the kitchen.

"You want take jam for your friend?" Lucy asked. "Peach."

"That would be nice, Lucy, thank you. But only two jars. I won't fit any more in my bag."

"I save some for Cap'n Daniel. Tell him you make." She laughed at her own joke. Lucy believed Emma and Daniel had a future together, but they both knew Emma's skills in the kitchen were limited.

Eleanor needed Emma's help in the stillroom for the rest of the day. Orders were flowing in for the herbal remedies now that the riverboats were out and about to deliver them.

"HERE IT COMES." Jacky Wirra turned to help Emma from the buggy before lifting out the box of herbals she was delivering to Dr. Wilson.

It was a few moments before Emma saw the glimmer of the coach lamps through the bush and heard the faint hoof beats and jingle of harness. As the four-horse team skittered to a halt beside them, the cloud of dust following, invisible in the dark, settled over everything. The driver's offsider lowered his rifle only slightly, wary of any danger lurking beyond their firelight.

Jacky handed her up, and the sleepy passengers stirred as Emma squeezed into the seat facing front. Her travelling bag and the box of herbals were added to the baggage on the back of the coach.

A crack of the whip and the horses were off again along the sandy track through the Mallee scrub. As they grew closer to their destination the track veered north, and the scrub gave way to towering river red gums. They forded the Murray River below the junction with the Darling and a mile further on crossed the Darling below the wharf spraying water from the wheels before rattling down the main street.

Two and a half hours after leaving Wirramilla Emma disembarked with the other passengers in front of the Wentworth Hotel, glad to stretch her legs and be done with the jostling and shaking. The passengers going on toward Adelaide hurried inside for a quick breakfast while the horses were changed at the livery stable.

Emma engaged a lad to carry the box of herbals and accompany her to Dr. Wilson's surgery further down the street. After delivering them and paying the lad, she set off for Catherine and Joe's house several streets away. A sharp wind chilled her hands and face and scattered leaves around her as she walked the dirt road.

"Hello, Sis. This is a pleasant surprise," Joe greeted her, peering out of the dining room as the maid let her into the hall. Emma could hear the wail of a small infant as she kissed her brother on the cheek. "You're just in time for breakfast. Esther, tell Mrs. Haythorne that Mrs. Berry is here, please."

Esther disappeared to do as she was bid, while Emma followed Joe into the dining room. Several covered dishes waited on the sideboard.

"To what do we owe this visit?" he asked sitting down again to his plate of scrambled eggs and bacon which her arrival had interrupted.

"You didn't receive my letter?"

"I might have done. Remind me."

Emma did so as she helped herself to toast and scrambled eggs and poured tea for them both.

"I remember now. So, you'll be staying here for a day or two first?"

Emma nodded, feeling the tea revive her. She much preferred the slow, smooth rhythm of river travel to the bumping and jostling of the coach.

"And how is my nephew?" she asked, as another wail reached them.

"Theo is doing well, thank you. Good lungs as you can tell. Doesn't like waiting for his meals."

The wail ceased, cut off in mid cry. Joe grinned tiredly. She wasn't surprised he had momentarily forgotten her letter.

"Emma, my dear, how are you?" Catherine bustled into the room, month-old Theo in her arms. She wore a silk wrapper printed with lilies and leaves in muted greens and purples, her blonde hair tied up in a bright purple scarf. Emma admired her vivacious style in notable contrast to her own mourning black. Her sister-in-law glowed with good health. "Come and say hello to your nephew."

Emma pushed her chair back and took the baby. She touched the soft, blonde fuzz on his head, looked into the dark eyes. "He's gorgeous."

Joe gazed at them, rapt. She realised she would be spending her time with babies and besotted parents for the next week or so. Deelie had six-week-old Orla as well as Brendan's little boy, Liam.

"I told cook to make enough breakfast for three this morning. I doubt you had eaten before you left. Is there anything else you'd like? More tea?"

"That would be lovely, thank you." Catherine went to fetch a fresh pot. "Catherine seems happy," Emma said. "And she remembered my letter."

Joe just smiled, his eyes on his infant son. He eventually tore himself away to his work at the Customs House.

"So," Emma said when she and Catherine were alone, "is Mrs. Keogh well enough to see me now?"

"It would seem so. I saw Dotty last week and she said her mother was feeling much better. She does have some scarring. I suspect that is what's been keeping her at home more than anything. Apparently when she does go out, she's taken to wearing a head-scarf that covers half her face."

"Poor woman."

Mrs. Keogh had contracted shingles, preventing Emma from speaking to her earlier about the old promise she and Matty Macdonald had made. Emma needed to convince the woman there was nothing between them now, or Mrs. Keogh wouldn't allow him to resume his courtship of her daughter.

Emma couldn't help feeling some irritation toward Matty. If he hadn't stopped seeing Dotty after Sam died – expecting Emma might want to honour that promise made to wed if they were both still single in ten years – he and Dotty could be married by now. Dotty would have taken over the household at Nettifield leaving Bea free to marry Thomas and get on with her own life.

"And how is Bea?" Catherine asked.

"Unhappy would be the best description I suppose." Emma sighed.

"I'm sorry Bea found out about the promise, Emma, but I couldn't see any other way of convincing Mrs. Keogh except to tell her the truth."

Bea hadn't forgiven her for keeping the promise a secret all those years. It didn't help that she was now caught up in the fallout. Emma had seen her friend and neighbour only once since January. She knew from Bea's younger brother Jim, that relations were strained between her and Matty as well. It was a mess all round.

"It's not your fault," Emma assured Catherine. "This started a long time before you even knew we all existed, and I do appreciate your help."

"I just hope you can work it out."

Emma heartily agreed.

Chapter 2

Facing Mrs. Keogh

DOTTY KEOGH opened the door to Emma's knock.

"Mrs. Berry?"

"Hello Miss Keogh. May I come in? I would like very much to speak to your mother if I possibly could."

Emma had chosen to turn up on the Keogh doorstep rather than risk a refusal to make an appointment to meet. As it was Wednesday half-day, she knew the Keogh's drapery store would be closed and took the chance they would be at home.

Dotty glanced behind her to an open door. "I don't know..."

"Bring her in, Dotty," Mrs. Keogh called from the adjoining room.

Dotty took Emma's coat and hat and hung them on the coat stand, and Emma followed her into the parlour, thinking this must be how people felt when called up for questioning during the Spanish Inquisition. It might not be her life at stake but through her both Bea and Matty had their lives on hold. She had to make it right.

The curtains in the Keogh's parlour were drawn and the room dim. Emma could just make out Mrs. Keogh, her back to the window, sitting on the sofa.

"Thank you for seeing me, Mrs. Keogh," Emma said, taking a seat in the armchair to which Dotty directed her. "I hope you are feeling better after your illness."

"As well as can be expected, I suppose, thank you."

"Can I get you tea?" Dotty asked.

"Do that," her mother said. "Our conversation won't take long," she added when Dotty had left the room, "but it gets her out of the way. So, Matty Macdonald has sent you to talk me around has he? I must admit he seems to have no shortage of women taking his part in this matter. You, your sister-in-law, his own sister. You all seem determined on his marrying Dotty. Makes me wonder a little why you are so keen to get him out from underfoot, so to speak."

This was going to be just as difficult as Emma had feared.

"While I am here on Matty's behalf," she said, "I am not here at his request, Mrs. Keogh. He has no knowledge of any of this. And secondly, I am attempting to set right a misunderstanding, a sequence of events that has led us to this point. May I elucidate?"

"I am agog to hear," Mrs. Keogh replied drily.

Emma clasped her clammy hands and dived in.

"So, you want me to believe," Mrs. Keogh said, when Emma finally stopped speaking, "that Matty Macdonald stopped seeing my Dotty because he was honouring the proposal he made to you to marry if you were both still single in ten years? And as you were now a widow and single again, and the time hadn't quite run out, he abandoned my Dotty to chase you up? That's your story, is it?"

"That is the way it happened," Emma said, though not quite comfortable with Mrs. Keogh's choice of words. "I didn't know for several months that Matty had stopped seeing Dotty after my husband's death. It certainly wasn't something I encouraged. But Matty is an honourable man, Mrs. Keogh. He made a promise to me and he kept it to the letter, regardless of his feelings for your daughter."

"Honourable is it, to break a girl's heart?"

"He felt I had a previous claim," Emma said beginning to feel desperate. "But we do not love one another. Not in that way. We are friends. Marrying isn't what either of us want now if we ever really did. It was a silly romantic idea at the time."

"So you say. I'm concerned his sister didn't know. It makes me rather doubt. Are you telling me you kept it secret all those years?"

"Pretty much. I did tell one family member about it, and Matty told his mother before she died. She wanted to see us marry then, but we didn't. If we didn't marry for her sake, you can surely see it wasn't something either of us really wanted."

"Mmm."

"Mrs. Keogh," Emma went on leaning forward, "I don't want Matty or Dotty to be unhappy because of a misunderstanding. If Matty makes a promise to Dotty, he will keep to it just as he did to me." She wondered if it was wise to make such a claim about another person, but she believed she knew Matty's nature.

There was a clatter of teacups as Dotty came back in with a tray. Emma wouldn't have been surprised if she had been listening. Conversation ceased as Dotty poured the tea and handed around the plate of biscuits.

"Will you be spending time on your riverboat this season, Mrs. Berry?" Mrs. Keogh asked.

The change of subject took Emma by surprise until she realised Mrs. Keogh was angling to know what Emma's plans were for herself, and if they had anything to do with Matty.

"Indeed. I'm on my way to visit the Lockwoods for a few days, but then my brother-in-law should be down with the *Mary B*. I am looking forward to it."

"The Lockwoods at River Bend?" Emma nodded. "I've met Mrs. Lockwood but it's her daughter Barbara I mostly see in the store. So many sons. You know them well, do you?"

Emma bit back a smile. "I've only met Mrs. Lockwood the once last year. I'm actually visiting a friend who is employed there."

The conversation turned to everyday matters and Mrs. Keogh made no further reference to the reason for Emma's visit. Eventually Emma stood to leave, feeling she had wasted her time. Mrs. Keogh was never going to change her mind about Matty Macdonald. Perhaps they were protesting too much.

"Thank you for listening to me, Mrs. Keogh," she began.

Mrs. Keogh winced and pressed her fingers to her forehead.

"Ma." Dotty immediately went to her and put her arm around her mother's shoulder.

"Do you have pain still from your illness?" Emma asked, as the woman sat with head bowed.

"I do," Mrs. Keogh replied, her voice thready. "I tire easily, and the store has been a concern. Dotty can't cope on her own."

Shingles pain could last a long time if there had been nerve damage. Emma could only hope for Mrs. Keogh's sake that wasn't the case. Worrying about her business wouldn't help.

"Do you have something to take for the discomfort?"

"I was using one of your grandmother's herbals, in fact, that I got from Dr. Wilson, but he is out of it."

"Would it have been the Indian hemp mixture?"

"It was."

"I delivered him a fresh supply this very morning. You must run up to the surgery and get another bottle, Miss Keogh."

"Oh, thank heaven. Please go at once, Dotty," Mrs. Keogh said, eyes closed as she massaged her forehead.

"I'm going, Ma," Dotty replied slipping out to the hall.

"Do you have rosemary growing in your garden?"

"Yes." Mrs. Keogh gave Emma a puzzled look through half-closed eyes.

"Miss Keogh," Emma stopped Dotty in the hall as the girl was buttoning her coat. "Can you pick some sprigs of rosemary before you go. It will provide your mother some relief in the meantime."

Dotty returned from the back garden in a few minutes with the rosemary and Emma instructed Mrs. Keogh to press it to her forehead and roll it gently back and forth. The woman sighed in relief as she did so.

"Is that better, Ma?"

"It is. Who would have thought?"

"Unfortunately, you have to keep doing that for it to be effective," Emma said. "But it is useful in the short term. You will be careful with the medicine Dr. Wilson has prescribed, won't you? Only take as much as he says. Too much can be dangerous, and you can always use the rosemary in between if you need."

"I'll make sure she does," Dotty said. "I'll mark the level on the bottle."

"That won't be necessary," Mrs. Keogh told her daughter tartly.

Emma wondered if Mrs. Keogh had overdone her dosage in the past, but she had said enough. The woman was leaning back relaxed, the rosemary moving soothingly beneath her fingers.

"Well, I hope you are feeling better soon. Thank you again for listening to me," Emma said, gathering up her reticule.

"Sit down, Mrs. Berry. Dotty run and get that medicine from the doctor, there's a good girl." Dotty threw a hopeful glance at Emma as she left the room. "I suppose I can't allow a youthful indiscretion to govern lives forever," Mrs. Keogh said as they heard the front door open and close. "I will allow Matty Macdonald to call on Dotty again. But…" A sound quickly quelled, as if a hand had been clapped over a mouth, alerted them to Dotty's lingering presence in the hall. "But I will be keeping a close watch," Mrs. Keogh went on raising her voice. "I would not want a repeat of his behaviour, you do understand."

"I don't think Miss Keogh would tolerate that either," Emma said, remembering Dotty's comment several months back.

"She's a sensible girl." Mrs. Keogh nodded. "You seem to have a high regard for the man, Mrs. Berry. I count that in his favour. With reservations, of course."

Not a woman to easily let go her original opinion, Emma decided. She met Dotty in the hall, hand on the doorknob, waiting. They went out together and started up the street.

"Thank you so much Mrs. Berry," Dotty said, her eyes shining, her step brisk. "You will let Mr. Macdonald know, won't you? It wouldn't be proper for me to write and tell him myself, would it?" Her gaze darted between Emma and the street ahead. "No. He will come and call though, won't he?" This last said with a small frown.

"I will make sure he knows," Emma promised, hoping now she hadn't interfered where she shouldn't. What if Matty had cooled off in the meantime? And was Dotty right for Matty and Nettifield? Not that she had any right to judge. Well, it was out of her hands now.

Dotty gave a little skip. How old was she? Eighteen, nineteen? No older certainly.

"Go," Emma said with a laugh, as the girl clearly needed to run and not just to fetch her mother's medicine.

Chapter 3

Reaching River Bend

THE SUN WAS shining but the breeze still held a chill when the livery stable buggy called for her at the appointed hour next morning. Tom Gulbis the stable owner, helped her into the buggy and made her comfortable with a rug over her legs before hauling his short, stout body into the driver's seat. Catherine waved to her from the front door as they set out.

Emma wasn't surprised to see the livery station owner driving her himself, rather than giving the job to an employee. Both his daughters were married to Lockwood brothers. He would no doubt visit with them while he was at River Bend.

The one-and-a-half-hour journey took them north up the Darling River along another sandy track through more Mallee scrub and red gums. As they neared their destination, the river fell away in a wide loop, and the scrub became lighter. As the river swung back toward them, the single-storey home-stead and farm buildings of River Bend came into sight, a timber-clad flour mill visible above the roof-tops, it's timber sails still.

Emma saw the women standing at the door of the homestead as her buggy rounded the corner between the homestead and the barn. They weren't looking at her arrival however, but at two men confronting one another in front of the mill more than a hundred yards away on a slight rise. The larger of the two shook his fist at the other man and shouted though she couldn't distinguish the words. She heard the other man shout something back. She shaded her eyes with her hand and squinted into the sun.

A third man came striding across and spoke to the combatants, sending the larger man into the mill and the other toward the homestead. She recognised the loose-limbed walk of the man heading down the rise. It was Brendan O'Neill.

The buggy had come to a halt and Mr. Gulbis helped her off.

"Hello, Tom," Mrs. Lockwood greeted him before turning to Emma. "Mrs. Berry, welcome to River Bend." She held out her hands. The woman hadn't changed since Emma had last seen her leaving Merrim Station on the steamer *Sapphire* all those months ago. She was still just as large and motherly looking, brown eyes warmly welcoming, grey hair in a loose bun at the back of her neck.

"It's so kind of you to invite me to visit with Deelie," Emma responded taking her hands.

A fat elderly beagle who had been sitting beside Mrs. Lockwood, lurched to her feet looking up at Emma a goofy smile on her face, tail wagging, as if agreeing to the welcome.

Mrs. Lockwood laughed. "This is Beauty. She's older than I am in dog years."

"She's very friendly," Emma said, bending to pet her.

"Wait until you meet her offspring," said the younger woman who was with Mrs. Lockwood.

"This is my daughter, Barbara."

Barbara Lockwood was somewhere near Emma's age, tall and slim, but with the dowdy dress of someone who didn't bother with how she looked. Her dark hair, pulled severely back, accentuated her face which was too long to be considered beautiful. There was nothing dowdy about the assessing look she gave Emma from her cool blue-grey eyes, though. What was she being sized up for?

"We go by first names only here," Barbara said with a smile, "otherwise you'd be Lockwooding us to eternity." Emma doubted she would call any of the Lockwood men by their first name should she meet them.

"I'm happy to meet you, Barbara, and I'm Emma.

"Right. Come along then," she said briskly. "I'll take you to Deelie's cottage. You'll get to meet the rest of the mob soon enough."

Mrs. Lockwood nodded to Emma. "We'll have a nice chat while you're here, m'dear."

Before Emma could take a step, her way was blocked by a tall well-built man in his mid to late thirties, clearly related to Barbara although a bushman's beard hid his chin and partly shortened his long face. His blue-grey eyes held no warmth, but Emma had the feeling that was normal for him and nothing to do with her. She recognised him as the man who had interrupted the argument at the mill.

"You can meet my brother Andrew right now, apparently," Barbara said, giving him an amused look.

"Mrs. Berry. Welcome to River Bend." His voice was hearty but no warmer than his eyes. "I'll be able to show you around later."

"That's – most thoughtful of you," Emma responded, a little uncertain as it hadn't sounded as if she had a choice in the matter.

"Tch. Give the girl a chance to get her breath, Andy. She's barely put foot on the place." Andrew Lockwood ignored his sister, continuing to stare at Emma. It was becoming uncomfortable. "Come along," Barbara said briskly turning away.

Emma nodded to Andrew and picked up her bag which Mr. Gulbis had left at her feet before disappearing and hurried after Barbara. The woman took a path around the further side of the homestead and through a large cottage garden full of plants Emma knew would flower come spring. A screen of eucalypt trees at the rear were underplanted with medium sized shrubs, grey honey myrtle and Mallee wattle. Hens clucked behind the greenery. A man was bending over a flower bed, a wheelbarrow half full of weeds and trimmings beside him.

"Brendan."

"Mrs. Berry. You're here, then."

"Emma, remember," she corrected him. "It's good to see you. You're looking well."

He had added a little weight to his medium height, light frame which did him no harm, and was due no doubt to a regular diet of Deelie's good cooking. His skin was tanned, his shock of black hair not making the same contrast to the pale skin she remembered.

Brendan said he'd see her at supper, and she went on aware of Barbara waiting for her. A sturdy wire mesh fence extended from the back corner of the homestead past the garden. Through a gate they entered a space where four cottages stood in an inward curving row overlooking a grassed area.

A double seat swing hung from a sturdy frame and buckets and spades marked a sandy patch. Small garden beds and several bench seats dotted around gave the space a welcoming feel.

"How pretty and inviting," Emma said, stopping to look. "Is this where your workers live?"

"No, no. Andrew and Ruth, and Declan and Naomi live in the first two cottages. The next one is empty." She glanced back at Emma as she said this.

"Declan is another of your brothers?" Barbara nodded. "Are he and Andrew the only ones married?" Barbara said they were, which meant the two wives, Ruth and Naomi, must be the Gulbis sisters. It was good to get it straight in her head. Emma wondered if the empty cottage was waiting for the next brother who got married. Or perhaps Barbara had hopes of making it hers.

The sound of children's voices caused Emma to look in the other direction to the area behind the homestead. Four young children were sitting with a woman under a huge weeping peppermint. There was a small building almost hidden behind it.

"That's the schoolhouse back there," Barbara explained. "We have a resident schoolteacher, Ann Russell. You'll meet her tomorrow with the rest."

Emma would have felt happy for Deelie and Brendan to be living here if she hadn't seen the altercation. Before they could move on, Emma was accosted by a friendly young dog.

"Hello, is this Beauty's little fellow?"

"Alfie. He's the children's dog. A right little rascal."

Alfie looked beagle-like, but his colouring wasn't standard and his legs were longer than the norm. She bent and ruffled his head behind his ears.

"He is a beagle, isn't he?"

"Mostly." Barbara laughed before moving on. Alfie trotted with them to the cottage at the far end. It was the smallest of the four.

"Deelie, your guest is here," Barbara called, knocking on the door.

There was a wail from inside and Deelie appeared after a moment, holding the front of her dress closed with one hand and a wailing Orla in the other. Her dark curly hair was tied loosely back and hung past her shoulders. Her blue eyes crinkled as she greeted Emma, who gave her an awkward hug trying not to crush the baby.

Barbara melted away, with a brisk, "I'll see you later."

"I have to finish feeding Orla," Deelie apologised. "You can freshen up in the washhouse out back. Your bed is in the sleepout. I shan't be long."

"Take your time," Emma said giving her another quick hug. "I'm here for a week."

Deelie hurried into the bedroom. Emma could hear young Liam chattering. She looked around. She was interested to see what accommodation the married workers at River Bend were given. The cottage had two main rooms, the bedroom, and the kitchen where she was standing. There was a faded armchair either side of the fireplace, a table with four mismatched wooden chairs, and a dresser against the far wall.

A pot stand in the corner and bins of flour and sugar beside a curtained bench under the window made up the cooking area. In the sleepout, she found Liam's bed and another one, her own she assumed. The cottage was a step up from Brendan's dirt-floored room in the stables at Merrim station.

Emma put her bag on the bed and took out a towel and wash things and headed to the washhouse. The small timber-clad shed was open on one side and fitted with concrete tubs, a copper, and a mangle. A tin bathtub hung on the wall, and an oilcloth curtain on the open side provided privacy when needed.

Emma turned on the tap over the tub and was rewarded with a steady stream of cold river water. What a boon that would be for Deelie. An outhouse adjoined at the end of the wash house and a rainwater tank held clean water for drinking and cooking. In the fully fenced backyard were several clotheslines, a large vegetable garden and some fruit trees. Beyond it was the ever-present Mallee scrub. This was almost luxurious accommodation for a farm labourer.

When she had freshened up, she found Deelie in the kitchen helping Liam to a drink of milk. The little boy was eighteen months old now, Brendan's boy by his first wife, Bridget, who had died over a year ago. The baby girl was in a basket, content after her feed. Emma did her duty and cooed over the dark haired infant. Not a patch on her nephew Theo but then she might be considered biased.

"You've named her Orla? Does it have any special meaning?"

Deelie smiled. "Golden princess. Her full name is Bridget Orla O'Neill. But I think when we register her birth, I might get Bren to drop the Bridget."

"Ah." She understood Deelie not wanting the ghost of Brendan's first wife hovering over her daughter. "You could always turn the names about."

Deelie nodded. "It's something we've to talk about." Emma felt that held more meaning than the simple words implied. She hoped there wasn't a problem in their marriage. It had been somewhat pressured, after all.

"I'm sure you'd like a cup of tea. You must be parched after the drive. I know I want one and the kettle is on the boil. Would you hold Liam while I make it? It's easier if he's not under foot."

Emma picked him up, and he wriggled and pushed at her to be put down again.

"Wheest, now, you'll not get a biscuit," Deelie warned him.

"Da," Liam said.

Deelie laughed. "It's always Da, never Ma." She reached down two cups and saucers from the dresser and stood with them in her hands. "I can't believe you're really here, Emma. It seems forever since we were at Merrim." She put the cups on the table.

"It does, doesn't it?" Emma agreed. "How is everything here? Do you like it?"

"Bren loves it. He gets to do different things, helping Rory in the smithy, gardening, working in the stable, fixing and mending. And not having to worry about Liam." Emma noticed Deelie didn't say how she felt.

Her friend took the teapot to the fireplace. Emma watched in amazement as she lifted a hinged fire screen to reach the kettle, lowering it into place again when she'd filled the teapot.

"Wherever did you get the fire screen? I've seen nothing to match that anywhere. How ingenious."

"It is that. Rory made it. This was one they had in their house, but they don't have small children, so they let me have it. He makes them for everyone. He'll be making another one for themselves soon though as Janet helps me with Liam at times."

"Rory? He's a blacksmith?"

"He is. We see a great deal of him and Janet. It's lovely having someone to talk to again." Deelie set the teapot on the table and opened a biscuit tin, putting shortbread biscuits on a plate and handing one to Liam. He at once tried to stuff it whole in his mouth. "These are her Scottish shortbreads."

Emma tried one. "Mmm."

"How is Daniel and everyone back at Wirramilla?" Deelie asked.

"They're all fine. Nella is expecting again, her fourth. I haven't seen Daniel for three months since the season ended but the water levels have risen, and trade has started. He'll be at Wentworth by the end of next week."

"And you're looking forward to being back on the *Mary B*?" Deelie asked, trying unsuccessfully to stifle a yawn.

"Do you usually have a nap at this time of day?" Emma knew enough about babies to understand how tiring they were.

"Well, yes but..."

"No buts. If I know anything, you sleep whenever you can get the children settled."

Deelie rubbed her eyes. "That's true enough, but Liam was crotchety, and I had to put him down earlier and now he's awake and Orla's ready to sleep." She looked as if she were close to tears, she was so tired. At least, Emma hoped that was the only problem. Deelie didn't seem her usual bright self but perhaps she was judging too quickly. An eighteen-month-old and an infant were bound to be a handful.

"Why don't I take Liam for a walk while you have a nap," Emma suggested. "Tire him out a little so he'll sleep well tonight. Would that help?"

"I can't expect you to do that. You've just got here." The protest was almost indignant as if what Emma had suggested broke all the rules of hospitality.

"I didn't come here to make more work for you, Deelie. Now off you go. Liam and I will be fine for an hour or so."

"Well, I won't complain," Deelie said yawning again. "You could visit with Janet over behind the smithy. It's at the far end of the barn."

"I'll find it," she said. This Janet might tell her what was going on with Brendan and the other man, too.

Chapter 4

Andrew Lockwood

LIAM LET HER take his hand and they set off at a slow pace across the grass. Alfie came running up making Liam squeal with delight as he bounced around them. The little dog slipped through the gate to the garden as Emma opened it and went racing off. Emma had a sinking feeling he shouldn't be out here. Too late now.

"Da, da," cried the boy, pulling away from Emma when he spied Brendan working in the garden.

"We're off to visit Janet at the smithy," Emma said as Brendan lifted Liam into his arms. "Deelie's having a rest. Is that little dog allowed out? He slipped through the gate when I opened it."

"Did he now?" Brendan replied. "I'll track him down before he gets into too much trouble. But come, I'll show you the way to Janet's cottage and introduce you."

Emma saw a bruise on the side of his face that she hadn't noticed before. "Is everything all right here?" she ventured as they walked.

"Sure, and all," the Irishman said. "Nothing to complain about. Deelie and me, we're right grateful for you getting us this place. How did you find our little cottage? Better than that room in the stable back at Merrim, now."

Exactly what Emma had thought herself but not what she meant by her question. They crossed the L-shaped open space created by the homestead and the barn. A man was working inside the barn at a bench, planing a length of timber. The sound of hammer on iron greeted them as they rounded the end of the building.

Brendan waved to a big, burly man in a leather apron hammering away in the open-fronted smithy. Further along was a door, marked with a potted geranium by the step. The woman who answered Brendan's knock was of mid height, shorter than Emma, and of slight build. She was probably a similar age of Mrs. Lockwood but looked more weathered. Her eyes lit up at the sight of Brendan and young Liam.

"This is Mrs. Berry who's come to visit," Brendan said, "and this is our good friend Janet, the better half of that rogue Rory who works the smithy."

"Call me Emma, please," Emma said.

"Janet Felling," the woman said her Scots brogue obvious, her brown eyes, flecked with gold, friendly enough. "Everything all right then, Bren?" she asked taking Liam from him.

"Nothing I can't handle. You didn't happen to spy that Alfie run by here by any chance?"

"Och, no." Janet shook her head. "Try over by the chicken coop."

"I will." Brendan nodded and walked away.

Janet held the door for Emma to come inside.

"Mrs. Berry." Andrew Lockwood appeared from the far side of the barn. "This is convenient. I can show you around right now."

Emma looked from Andrew to Janet and back, about to tell him it wasn't convenient at all when she felt Janet's touch on her arm.

"I'll take care of young Liam," the older woman said with a nod of encouragement. "Come by and we'll have that tea when you're done."

"You'll want to see over the mill," Andrew said as he led the way up the rise.

Emma hadn't seen a flour mill before and she was interested, though she wasn't sure why Andrew wanted her to see it. Did he feel competitive with other pastoralists? She found herself struggling to keep up with him as he strode up the rise. What was she rushing for anyway? She slowed to a more comfortable pace and let him get ahead. The mill rose before her, dwarfing all. She paused to take it in. It was impressive, reminding her of a giant pepper pot. Huge canvas covered sails, still now, dominated. Andrew was waiting for her when she reached the top of the rise. His face conveyed neither warmth nor annoyance at her tardiness.

"Flour milling will be big business once men realise wheat farming is the way to go out here," he said.

It sounded like an announcement he had made often. Emma considered that her father, like many other pastoralists, did very well with sheep, thanks to the riverboats that transported the wool to market.

"See here." Andrew pointed out a brick building under construction about fifty yards further along the rise, the river curving around behind. Several men were laying bricks from a platform. Emma hadn't noticed it when she arrived her attention being on the men arguing in front of the mill. "That's our new steam-powered flour mill," Andrew explained. "With steam power we can work all hours instead of depending on the vagaries of the wind."

"I see," Emma said feeling impelled to respond. "I can understand the attraction of that sort of efficiency. What are you going to do with the old mill? It's quite an impressive building."

"It will make good firewood for the steam mill," Andrew replied with satisfaction.

Emma tried to hide her surprise. She suspected Andrew Lockwood didn't take kindly to having his ideas questioned and who was she, a visitor, to do so anyway. But the building could be put to better use than firewood surely.

"What about the machinery? Will you be putting that in the new mill?" she asked.

"No, no. All new except for the millstones. We'll re-use those. Our blacksmith will make good use of the old workings." Emma, reminded of Deelie's fire screen, didn't doubt it. "I'll show you over."

They entered the base of the mill. The space, as Emma stepped in, felt oppressive with heavy supporting timbers. A man was working there sewing up bags of flour. He was solid in build, dressed in moleskin trousers, a leather jerkin open over his shirt, sleeves rolled to the elbow. A dusting of flour covered him from his flat cap down to his boots. Emma recognised him as the man who had been shouting at Brendan, but it was the leer on his dark jowly face as he spied her that distinguished him.

"Well, what 'ave yer got yersel' here then, Andy?" he said roughly in an accent Emma placed as belonging to northern England.

Emma glared at him and turned to Andrew Lockwood, expecting a reprimand for the man's rudeness.

"Have you fixed the broken slat on that sail yet Brighten?" Andrew asked. "No? Go do it now. We want to get in a full day's work tomorrow to make up for yesterday."

"Huh!" the man stabbed the needle and twine into the top of the flour bag and stomped out, causing Emma to step aside quickly.

No apology was forthcoming as Andrew Lockwood explained to Emma how the flour came down the chute from the grinding stones on the upper level.

"You put a bag under the chute to catch the flour. The bags of wheat are hauled to the upper floor using the same wind power that turns the stone."

Emma put her hand in the wooden tub and rubbed flour between her fingers. "This is wholemeal with the husk still in?"

"Yes. But if we put a sieve at the end of the chute, we can catch the husks and get fine white flour anytime we need to," he said as if her query had been a criticism.

Emma brushed the flour from her fingers. "May I see up top?" So long as she was here, she may as well see it all. She felt she knew all she wanted about Andrew Lockwood and Mr. Brighten.

He took the open ladder-like steps two at a time. Emma followed more slowly holding up her skirt, her free hand on the wall as there was no handrail. As she neared the top, Andrew bent and grasped her arm. Her chest tightened.

What had she been thinking? She'd put herself in a vulnerable position alone at the top of the mill with a man she had just met and didn't particularly like. An image of the miller's leering face flashed through her mind. Daniel was always telling her she was too careless of her personal safety, trusting in herself.

Andrew tugged and she had no choice but to step onto the upper level. He released her arm as if it burnt. She stepped smartly away from him and the coldness gripping her chest eased, but she remained on her guard. Looking around, she tried to appear as if the mill was wholly occupying her thoughts. The place did have its effect. The first thing she was aware of was the machinery crowding the space, and the huge millstones. No wonder it needed the heavy timbers she had seen below. The second thing was the view.

There were four openings with shutters that could be closed against the weather. Through them one got a bird's-eye view of the countryside and the River Bend property. Emma had been on the upper floor of hotels before, but they hadn't given this impression of height. Here you could see in every direction just by turning your head.

Andrew Lockwood hadn't moved. He stood near the top of the ladder where she had left him, his face expressionless, his eyes as cold as when he had introduced himself. The man didn't appear to have a drop of passionate feeling in his body unless it was for his mill.

Through the window opening to the north Emma could see miles of the Darling River curving away in the distance. As she looked a sail moved past the opening startling her.

"Oh. It isn't working, is it?"

"Of course not. Brighten is turning the sails so he can get to the one needing repair," Andrew said as if it were self-explanatory.

Suitably chastened she moved to the next opening. This showed the whole of the long loop of river that comprised the eastern part of the Lockwood property. Down at the furthest point, a patch of ordered rows in autumn colours interspersed with strips of dull green caught her eye.

"What is that down there?" Emma asked. "Is it an orchard?"

Andrew moved to stand behind her. She held herself tightly trying to ignore his presence.

"That is Evan's little project. He'd like to have that whole area planted with vines watered from the river."

His dismissive tone seemed to put paid to Evan whoever he was. One of his many brothers perhaps. Emma wondered if the Darling River would support a vineyard. It was notorious for spending the summer as a string of pools rather than a stream, unlike the Murray which fed the vineyards at Albury reliably enough. The Barossa Valley vineyards had their own river and creek system.

"Perhaps a dam," she murmured.

Andrew didn't respond and she moved away to the third opening. This one looked over the barn, homestead, and cottages. She could see Brendan still working in the garden, and a plump woman with a child in her arms walking toward the second cottage. Ruth or Naomi perhaps. She was relieved to see the dog Alfie bounding around the woman. Brendan must have got him back in the yard.

It occurred to her that Andrew Lockwood could keep a watch on everyone from this eerie. She could imagine him standing here taking note of what they were all doing. He would have his eyes on her now when she moved about the place. Her skin prickled. It wasn't a pleasant thought.

"How many men does it take to work the mill?" Emma asked, deciding she should show some interest in the workings.

"Two at best. One up here putting the wheat into the stones and one below bagging the flour. It can be done by one going up and down as needed, but that's not as efficient when you must rely on the wind. When it changes direction the cap and the sails need to be turned to take best advantage."

He explained a little more about the machinery, but Emma found herself drawn again to the view as she moved to the last opening. She was probably confirming Andrew Lockwood's low opinion of a woman's intelligence in doing so. She was sure he had one.

"But what has happened here?" A section of the wall was blackened and scorched. She touched it and her fingers came away smudged with black. "It's fresh. You had a fire here recently?"

She knew flour milling was dangerous. Flour dust was highly flammable and could explode in a fireball if there was enough of it in the air.

"Just a slight mishap," he assured her. "A nail got lodged between the stones and caused a spark. The fire was quickly doused."

"I've read newspaper reports of fires in flour mills. I'm not sure my father would want something as dangerous at Wirramilla."

"Greatly exaggerated," Andrew said dismissing the claim out of hand. "I would argue that flour milling is safer than traveling on a riverboat. I've heard stories of how they catch on fire from sparks from the funnel, not to mention sinking, running aground, men drowning." Emma went cold. Was he referring to the sinking of the *Mary B* and Sam's death? Not a nice man to bring it up that way. She wasn't sure he understood social niceties.

"Are you interested in the riverboat trade, Mr. Lockwood?" Emma asked, her voice cool.

"Is it a profitable business?"

Emma turned to look at him. "I beg your pardon?"

"I'd like to know, in general," Andrew said. "There seem to be a great number of boats on the rivers now. I presume they wouldn't be there if they weren't making a living, but I don't know. Perhaps they just survive hand to mouth."

"It's a decent living, yes." They did owe some monies on the *Mary B* still, but another good season would see that cleared. How soon they could clear Mr. Knowles' ten percent ownership was another matter and not one she was prepared to discuss with Andrew Lockwood.

"You work on the boat, don't you?"

Emma felt a prickle at the back of her neck. Had he heard rumours about her relationship with Daniel? He seemed to be well informed on her life. Why, she had no idea, but it was making her decidedly uncomfortable.

"As second officer," Emma replied. "It's a family business after all."

"Hardly something a woman would be able to carry off," he said dismissively, "but your brother-in-law would be the one with the authority."

She drew a calming breath. His opinion didn't matter to her, not really. She wasn't here to impress the Lockwoods. Emma turned back to look out the last opening toward the west and the Anabranch, the ancient bed of the Darling its edging of gum trees hazy on the horizon. Somewhere between here and there, she knew, were the Lockwood flocks under the care of shepherds.

"It's respect that matters," she said, thinking of what she had dealt with on their last journey, "not family connections."

Andrew Lockwood was silent for a moment. She didn't know if he was considering her response or lost in his own thoughts.

"Owning a riverboat," he said, "or at least an interest in one, would be useful for us to have. We could send flour and other produce to the markets whenever we chose. Put us ahead of the competition. I intend having the finest flour going."

"I see." Did he expect her to say more? He could have asked any riverboat captain at the Wentworth wharf for the information and more, she had given him.

"If you've seen enough..."

"Oh, yes. Thank you. I must get back and collect Liam."

The tension in her shoulders eased once she found herself out in the open again. Andrew Lockwood gave her a curt nod and walked off toward the brick mill under construction. It appeared she had reached the end of her tour of inspection. A sound above caused her to look up. Mr. Brighten was standing on a ladder working on the sail. She hoped she wouldn't meet him again while she was here. She didn't care if she never had any further contact with Andrew Lockwood either.

Chapter 5

Something's Troubling Deelie

JANET FELLING welcomed her in when Emma knocked on her door. She had scrubbed the black soot from her fingertips with her handkerchief wetted with a little spit. The handkerchief was going to need seven days in the sun to restore it to its original snowy whiteness.

"How did your tour with Mr. Andrew go?" Janet asked, pouring Emma's tea while Liam claimed another biscuit, his plate already dotted with crumbs. Janet Felling's kitchen was warm and welcoming with a kettle singing on the hob and gingham curtains at the window, a matching cloth on the round table. It was a pleasant contrast to the feeling at the mill.

"Does he show everyone over the mill who visits?" she asked.

"Oh, no. Not everyone, hen. Not everyone." Janet sipped her tea but didn't elaborate.

"There was a man working in the mill when we went in. Brighten, I think his name is. I saw him arguing with Brendan when I arrived. I hope there isn't a problem there." Janet gave her a quizzical look. The woman was probably thinking she was being nosy. "It's just that I was the one who arranged for Deelie and Brendan to come here," she hastened on. "I'd hate to think I'd put them into a bad situation."

"You'd have to ask Brendan about that," Janet said. "Jack Brighten is the man. He's a master miller. Andrew got him cheap after he was dismissed from his previous place. Always looking to the main chance is Andrew." She gave a wry smile. "He might be a Scot the way he watches his purse."

Liam held out his hand, imploring for another biscuit.

"No more, lad." Janet said. Liam let out a wail and flipped his plate over.

"I think it's time I took you back home," Emma said. "I hope Deelie's had enough sleep."

Janet chuckled. "There's no such thing when you have young bairns," she said.

"No, I suppose not. Thank you for the tea and biscuits, and for taking care of Liam. I hope I see you again while I'm here."

"You'll see me at lunch tomorrow, don't worry about that. Everyone has lunch at the homestead."

"Oh, I see. Deelie did say something about lunch but I didn't get a chance to ask about it. I guess that's where I'll meet the rest of the mob then, as Barbara referred to them."

"Well, the women and children at least, for the time being."

Once outside, Liam wriggled to get down and Emma obliged despite the slow pace. She had nothing to hurry for, anyway. Deelie could sleep a little longer. The sky, clear earlier, was clouding over. It might rain tomorrow.

"I'm going to lose another whole season, Andy." The voice reached her as they were passing the barn. She paused, bending down as if attending to Liam, curiosity getting the better of her. "It'll take months to get the new trellises in, and I'll miss another planting season. A few extra rows aren't going to cut it. I need acres. If I could just hire some help I could have it set up in no time."

She recognised Andrew's voice as he answered. "I can't do it before the new mill is up and running, you know that. Another season won't matter in the long run."

Something clanged loudly. Liam let out a wail. She picked him up and hurried on, not daring to look behind but imagining eyes boring into her back whether they were or not. It seemed things weren't all smooth going at River Bend.

"WELL NOW, this is good to see." Emma said as she and Deelie returned to the kitchen after washing up the supper dishes in the washhouse tub. Brendan had his books out and was practising his letters at the kitchen table. One of the problems the pair had encountered in trying to leave Merrim Station was neither could read or write to apply for other positions.

"Young Ian Lockwood is teaching me," Brendan told her. Ian, he explained, was the youngest Lockwood brother at nineteen, and an artist.

Brendan himself was handy with a pencil sketch, as Emma had discovered during their time at Merrim, so she realised he and Ian had that in common. Right now, she admired his neatly executed letters. It put her own handwriting to shame.

"I brought some things for you both," she said. "I'll just fetch them."

"Emma," Deelie remonstrated as Emma headed for the sleepout.

"Ssh. You'll wake Liam. What sort of guest would I be if I didn't bring some thank you gifts for my hosts?"

She went quietly into the room coming back with a small pile of clothes, the two jars of Lucy's jam, and a book.

"I know you might not be ready to read this yet, Brendan, but you will be soon enough, and I loved it as a child." Emma handed him a copy of *The Swiss Family Robinson*.

"Emma, this is very generous of you. This is a rich gift." Brendan ran his hands over the still bright paper jacket. "I can't wait to read it. Liam will thank you for it later, too. Ian has promised to lend me some of his books. Perhaps I can lend him this one if he doesn't have it already. You are a dear friend."

"You are most welcome. Friendship goes two ways. You gave me enormous help at Merrim and helped keep me sane." Emma placed the clothes and the jam on the table. "Lucy sends you some peach jam, Deelie, and I have some dresses here," she said hoping it didn't sound as if she were giving charity. She had carefully selected items from her wardrobe that Deelie might like and find useful. "They will need only a little altering." Deelie was some four inches shorter, but about the same build. "And this cotton dress could be cut up to make a dress or two for Orla when she's a little older, and there's some grosgrain ribbon here for trim."

Deelie lifted the items one by one, remarking on how much she liked them. She ran her hand over a wool skirt in a warm chocolate colour with a patterned panel in various shades of brown and green near the hem.

"Oh, this is beautiful. This is fine to wear now with the weather cooling." She held it up against herself. "How can I shorten it without losing the panel?" she mused.

Emma looked at it and her heart sank. She should have given more thought to what she considered suitable. The effect of the design would be lost if the hem were simply raised.

"I'll have to take a piece off at the waist," Deelie decided. "That means unpicking the waistband and reshaping the top, but it would be worth it. I need to put it against another skirt to get the measurements." She patted her stomach. "Not as slim as I used to be." She disappeared into the bedroom.

Brendan looked up from the illustrations he was perusing in *The Swiss Family Robinson*. "It's good to see her smiling."

Emma wanted to ask him if Deelie was unhappy, but the girl came back out with a cotton skirt in her hand before she had the opportunity. She would find a way to ask Deelie later. Brendan's comment made her more certain that something wasn't right, however comfortable their surroundings.

Deelie spread the wool skirt on the table and overlaid it with her cotton skirt, carefully matching the length. From the corner cupboard she took out her sewing box and after some contemplation cut off a top portion of the wool skirt.

"Can I unpick the waistband for you?" Emma offered. "My needlework comes somewhere near my cooking and neither is my favourite occupation, but I am able to unpick. I've plenty of practice at that."

Deelie laughed. "That would be a great help. I can start taking in these side seams to shape the top."

She wielded her tape measure and placed pins where needed and was soon stitching away with some brown thread while Emma worked at the unpicking. Behind them the fire crackled and shed a warm glow. Brendan was absorbed in his new book. Emma wasn't sure how much of it he was able to read as he frowned over the words, but she was pleased with the reception of her gifts. Their value lay in the need of the recipient and she had tried to address that.

"I'm thinking I'll ask Janet to help with the fitting of the other dresses," Deelie said, interrupting Emma's thoughts. "She can help me with them after you've gone back home."

"That's a good idea. It's impossible to fit yourself properly. Every time you bend down to pin the hem it moves."

Deelie laughed. "It does that."

Emma laid a strip of fabric on the table. "There, I've finished with the waistband. How would a cup of tea go before bed?"

"Sounds like a fine plan," Brendan replied, yawning, and closing his book. Deelie kept her head down over her work and only stopped when the cup of tea was put in front of her. She would have gone on with her sewing after drinking it, but Brendan handed her a candle.

"You need your sleep," he said to her.

Emma could see Deelie was eager to be wearing the new skirt. She would try to take some chores off her friend's hands in the morning and give her time for sewing.

<><><>

SOMETHING was tapping at Emma's face. She tried to swipe it away and heard a giggle. She opened her eyes to see Liam staring at her, his fingers poised.

"Cheeky," she said, and made a grab for his hand. He leapt back, stumbled, and fell to the floor. His mouth opened about to cry. Emma grabbed him up and plopped him into bed with her.

"Shh, shh. You'll wake Orla." She tickled him until he laughed instead. There was subdued light at the edges of the canvas blinds. Somewhere after six. The air was a little warmer, and Emma wondered if the rain that had been threatening the day before would materialise.

She took Liam into the kitchen. She was about to give him a slice of bread spread with the peach jam but found a jar of plum jam already open and used that instead. She lit the fire. Brendan must have set it before he went to bed, and the kettle was full when she lifted it. Some warm water for washing and a cup of tea were the first orders of the day.

"This isn't the way guests are supposed to behave," Deelie said later, sipping the tea Emma put in front of her, Orla on her arm, a warm shawl across her shoulders. Brendan had already gone off to work.

"You know I don't need to be waited on, and you already have your hands full. What else would a friend do?"

"It does remind me of when we were at Merrim." Deelie paused as if looking back.

"You don't regret leaving there, do you?"

"Oh no. Don't bother yourself on that score. I don't miss Mr. Fraser or that misery Mort. No place is perfect, but it is better here. It's lovely to be able to chat over lunch every day."

She kept her face averted as she adjusted Orla's blanket. At Merrim she had been the only woman once the Andersons had left but Emma could tell everything wasn't rosy here whatever the benefits.

"Have you heard from your family lately?" she asked spreading jam on some toast for herself.

"No, but Janet wrote a nice letter for us at Christmas telling them where we were and everything, so I expect we'll hear something soon enough if our Ryan's boys are up in their lettering."

Emma hoped that would be the case. Deelie's family back in Ireland hadn't had word of her for over two years. She realised she knew nothing of Brendan's background apart from losing his first wife after Liam's birth.

"My fingers are itching to get on with my skirt," Deelie said, as she rushed through the morning chores with Emma's help.

Those done, she took up her sewing and they went to sit on the bench seat out front that looked down the length of the space in front of the cottages. Alfie came to join them, and he and Liam were soon rolling and falling over one another with much enjoyment for both it seemed.

Clouds continued to gather on the horizon. Up on the rise, Emma could just make out the top of the mill through the trees. Good to his word, Andrew had the mill working the sails turning briskly in the breeze, the rumbling clack of the cog wheels and whirr of machinery reaching them. She saw a movement close by through the greenery and heard the clucking of a hen. Someone was collecting the eggs from the chicken coop.

They hadn't been out long when a short plump woman appeared on the front porch of the furthest cottage. She looked their way before going back inside her cottage.

"Who was that?"

"Ruth, Andrew's wife," Deelie told her in a non-committal voice.

A few minutes later Ruth reappeared carrying a baby basket and came toward them.

"Hello, I'm Ruth," she introduced herself to Emma, ignoring Deelie. "And this is Ophelia." The baby looked about six months old and was playing with a rattle. Up close, Ruth had a pretty, round face and brown eyes, but a mouth that looked as if it could pout.

"I'm happy to meet you," Emma said getting to her feet. "I'm Deelie's friend, Emma Berry. Won't you take this seat, Ruth? I'll bring out a chair."

"Well, of course I know who you are," Ruth trilled as if Emma were particularly stupid. "We all do."

Emma was tempted to sit down again and leave the woman to stand but better manners prevailed. When she came out with the chair, Ruth was staring at nothing and Deelie had her head down over her sewing. She didn't think a word had been spoken between them in the minutes she had been gone. Alfie stuck his head in the baby's basket and Ophelia banged her rattle on his nose, surprising him and sending him back to Liam.

"Mother Lockwood has asked me to host an afternoon tea for you today," Ruth said to Emma.

"That's very kind of you," Emma said, wondering if she could politely refuse and remembering she hadn't been successful at doing that yesterday with Ruth's husband. "But I'm trying to look after Liam so Deelie can get more sleep. You know how hard that is with a new baby and a toddler."

As she spoke, Ophelia began to scream. Liam was waving the rattle. Emma took the toy from Liam and gave it back to the baby, stopping one child's cries but starting up another.

"Come on now," Emma told Liam, herding him back to the sandpit. "You're too big for rattles. Rattles are for babies and you're a big boy."

It seemed to work. He quietened down as she set him to digging with a little wooden spade. Alfie sat and watched keeping his distance from the spade it seemed, having already had a run in with the rattle.

"But it's fine, you going to afternoon tea, Emma," Deelie assured her when she returned to her seat. "You're supposed to be on holiday."

"We'll see you at three o'clock," Ruth said. "Ann, our schoolteacher, will come by when she finishes classes, and Evan will be there. But you mustn't ask Evan about his plans for the vineyard," she added in a conspiratorial whisper.

"Oh? Your husband pointed it out to me when he was showing me over the mill yesterday," Emma replied. She saw Liam pick up something in the sandpit and grabbed his hand in time to stop him putting it in his mouth. It was a silver boot button. She dropped it into her jacket pocket. "I thought it was Evan's project?"

"It is. But it is also a sore point with him because he can't develop it just yet. Poor boy is very touchy about it. It wouldn't pay to upset him. Just a friendly warning."

Emma had no time to ponder Ruth's remark. She was never sure which came first: the roar, or the fire ball rising above the trees. The sound louder than any thunderclap seemed to shake the ground, and the red flash lit the sky sending the birds screeching and swooping in fright as they fled.

In the eerie aftermath, Emma heard a strange thudding and clacking; things falling and hitting the ground like heavy rain. She could no longer see the top of the windmill, nor the sails.

Chapter 6

The Mill Explodes

EMMA RAN, aware as she did so of others rushing out of the cottages and the homestead, screams and cries of distress mixing with the roar of the flames. The scene that met their shocked gaze was like something from a hell.

The mill was ablaze, twisted machinery ghostly in the shattered remains. Flaming debris littered the ground on the rise, the broken sails hanging awkwardly, tangled in the branches of a gumtree at the end of the garden, launched off their spindle by the explosion.

A young man lay on the ground amid the outskirts of the burning debris, an easel fallen on top of him. Blacksmith Rory Felling was picking his way through the burning timbers. He plucked up the lad as if he were a baby and carried him down to the sofa on the front verandah where the women stood, horrified and helpless.

Barbara rushed to support the lad as Rory put him down on the bench seat beside the kitchen door, his head lolling sideways, blood on the side of his face.

"We need the doctor," Barbara shouted.

Several men were trying to get close to the mill, but the fierce fire kept them back. There was not going to be any rescue.

"Where's Andy? Has anyone seen Andy?" a man cried, running from behind the barn, a hint of hysteria in his voice.

A woman's scream startled Emma from her horrified contemplation of the scene. She turned and saw Ruth Lockwood, hands to her face, horror in her eyes.

"Ruth, come sit here with Ian," Barbara ordered. "If no one else is going for the doctor, I will."

"I can go," a man's voice responded from nearby.

Emma thought he was one of the men working on the brick mill building. There was a trickle of blood running down one side of his face. He sprinted away to the horse paddock past the barn. His offer was welcome, but it was probably tinged with a need to escape the horror too. It would be several hours before he returned from the ten mile ride to Wentworth, even if Dr. Wilson were immediately available.

A man, one of the brothers Emma thought seeing the long, bearded face, ran from the barn with a pole laden with clanking metal buckets shouting for everyone to lend a hand. She thought he was the one who run shouting from behind the barn. The women raced to join the line that the men were already forming, passing buckets of water up from the river as if it had been rehearsed a hundred times. Perhaps it had. It was something to do even if it would have little effect.

Tension was thick in the air, but no one panicked. The flames were roaring, fanned by the gusting southerly wind. There was danger of sparks being blown into the trees lining the river. The whole place could go up if the eucalypts caught. Mrs. Lockwood was doing a roll call of her sons as she stood near the top of the bucket line.

Harold Lockwood answered from further up the line to where Emma stood, and Frank almost immediately below past the little maid beside her. It was Frank who had run out of the barn with the buckets. Declan Lockwood's answer to his mother sounded from somewhere up nearer the mill.

"Evan's down at the vineyard," someone called out when he didn't answer to his name. A female voice answered for Ian. Barbara. Ian must be the one who had been knocked down. Andrew Lockwood failed to respond to his name call.

"Wasn't it today Andy was supposed to be going around the shepherds?" Frank shouted. Hopefully, Emma thought, when no one answered.

Emma couldn't see the miller anywhere, but no one was asking about his whereabouts. That was being taken as a given since the mill had been working. Where was Brendan? Did he ever work in the mill? Her throat closed at the thought.

She stepped out and turned, looking up and down the line. There he was. Down by the river next to the woman she had seen run out of the second cottage. That must be Naomi, Declan's wife. She looked much like her sister. Frank glared at her as he handed a full bucket to the maid and she quickly stepped back into place to take it in her turn.

Two men missing. There would be no survivors from that inferno. What they were doing right now was just mitigating the damage and the threat of anything worse. She hoped Ian would be all right. The trees above them whispered and swayed in the fitful breeze. It had been a good day for the mill to operate.

Emma wasn't sure how long they worked, passing full buckets up and empty ones down. She had to take several steps to meet the person on either side. Her arms and legs ached as passing along was also passing uphill. Up from the riverbank, over the bank of the intervening dry billabong, up the rise to the fire.

She couldn't see what was going on at ground level, the bank of the billabong restricting her view, but she could see the flames in the mill shooting upward. They didn't seem to be diminishing. The water was probably turning to steam before it even reached the burning wood. Still, they had to try.

Some of the buckets they were hauling up were only half full, others sloshed water on the ground and over her feet as she struggled to carry them. The maid who was beside her barely came up to Emma's shoulder and looked about to collapse. Barbara came down and took a place between them.

"How is Ian?" Emma asked as she passed down an empty bucket.

"Barely conscious. Deelie's sitting with him now."

Nothing more was said. Talking required energy. Frank Lockwood kept exhorting everyone to hurry. The brother who had answered to the name of Harold, this one cleanshaven, broke from his place up ahead in the line and came down.

"No amount of rushing is going to change anything, Frank." He looked up at the women above him, grimly toiling. "They're going as fast as they can."

A harsh sob escaped Frank's throat. His brother patted him on the back and took the place next to him. Everyone moved up a few steps as the buckets continued. Emma could feel blisters coming up on her hands. Her hair was escaping its pins and falling over her face. Her back was beginning to ache.

The wind dropped and smoke and soot drifted down to them, stinging their eyes. It came with a smell that sent some people retching. Then the rain that had been threatening came, tentative to start with then heavy, dropping gallons of water on the flames in moments.

With relief, Emma joined the rest of the women as they tramped wet and weary up to the homestead. She wasn't the only one bearing the marks of their toil. Hair loose, clothing bedraggled, wet and smoky, they looked a sorry lot. The fire in the mill might be soon under control but there was nothing to celebrate.

Standing under the shelter of the verandah, the women watched silently as the rain spittered and spat on the hot embers, gradually wearing down the flames, the quiet only punctuated by a woman sobbing quietly and another voice soothing. Ruth, Andrew's wife, now widow, was standing off to one side. She was being comforted by Janet and a slim, sharp faced young woman with an upturned nose. Her severe black skirt and jacket and white blouse suggested she was Ann Russell, the schoolteacher.

Both she and Janet showed signs of having been on the bucket line. Deelie was on the sofa, cradling Orla in one arm and Ian in the other, his head on her shoulder, Liam quiet at her feet. Several wide-eyed children were sitting on the verandah floor.

Mrs. Lockwood, her face grey and drawn, dropped heavily onto the arm of the sofa beside Ian. She put her arms around him, drawing his bloodied head from Deelie's shoulder to her own breast as she bent over him.

An older woman Emma hadn't seen before, put a comforting hand on Mrs. Lockwood's shoulder. She was taller than Mrs. Lockwood, with a big-boned frame and capable hands. Her grey hair hadn't dared come loose from its fastenings and was pulled firmly back from a face that fit the body. Despite the angularity, there was softness in her gaze. Beside her, Beauty the beagle leaned against Mrs. Lockwood's leg, offering her own form of comfort.

The men, oblivious of the rain, walked and poked about the building, steam and smoke now pouring out of what remained. Frank seemed particularly distressed, brushing at his eyes. She could have put that down to the smoke if she hadn't heard him earlier. He was the one shouting for Andy. He was the shortest of the Lockwood men she noted.

A loud creak from the mill was greeted with cries of alarm and shouted warnings, nerves already stretched. As they watched, the lower millstone parted from its mate with a screech and a crack of breaking timber, sending a billow of sparks and ash into the air. The upper millstone hung for a moment before following with a crash. Emma doubted they would be using them in the new mill.

A strangled sob broke from Mrs. Lockwood. The silence that followed spoke louder than words. The bodies of the two men were in the mill remains somewhere among the burnt timbers and bent machinery. It didn't bear thinking about.

"If we stay out here, we're all going to catch a chill and people still have to eat," said the older woman a quaver in her voice. "Come along girls. Gladys," she called as the maid Emma had been working beside on the bucket chain hung back, her eyes still on the mill. Or perhaps it was the men she was watching.

"Coming, Mrs. Fowler," Gladys whispered, and let herself be herded along the verandah to a side door with two other maids.

"Rory," Barbara called. "Can we get Ian into his bed, please. And Ann, take the children in for something warm and comforting."

The sharp-faced Ann objected. "I was going to stay with Ruth."

"Janet can do that for the moment, if you wouldn't mind, Janet? I need to see to Ian until the doctor gets here, and you need to see to the children."

Ann didn't look happy that her position beside the new widow had been usurped, but this was hardly a time for arguing. Naomi called the children to her, and she and Ann followed Mrs. Fowler and the maids to the kitchen. Emma was surprised Naomi wasn't comforting her sister as Barbara and Mrs. Lockwood disappeared inside with Rory and Ian.

People were moving, but there was a feeling of unreality. The grey sky and the rain seemed a fitting background to the atmosphere of shock and grief. Standing there now just felt ghoulish, and Mrs. Fowler was right. The chill was creeping in through Emma's damp clothes. With nothing else she could do to help and feeling more like an intruder on the family's grief, Emma picked up Liam and went back with Deelie to their cottage.

<><><>

THE LUNCH bell sounded later than usual according to Deelie. Emma found it surprising it had rung at all. Apparently, everyone had lunch at the homestead every day except Sunday. It made sense when most of those living there were family, she supposed. She wondered if it also meant a lower wage for those employed. Brendan opened the homestead's back door to them.

"Thought I might catch you," he said, giving Deelie a kiss on the cheek. He took Orla's basket from her. "Are you all right?" Deelie nodded. "Come, then. Lunch is ready."

The back door opened into the vestibule, which was dominated by a long table. An open door at the far end gave a view into the kitchen. Brendan disappeared into the house proper, through another door to the side where Emma could just see the end of a dining table through the doorway

Deelie and Emma took seats at the near end of the table in the vestibule. At the far end nearest the kitchen, Naomi Lockwood sat with four children, three girls and a boy, the oldest about eight. She was serving them food from several platters while Ann Russell sat nearby with a child about Liam's age on her lap. Barbara and Mrs. Lockwood were absent. The mood was sombre, even the children were quiet. Janet joined Deelie and Emma at the table.

"How is Ruth?" Emma asked her.

"Sleeping. I gave her some laudanum."

"And Ian?"

"Doctor hasn't arrived yet," she reported. "Something hit him really hard. He has a gash on the side of his face and lost a piece of his ear too, it seems."

"Oh, my goodness," said Deelie. "I do hope he'll be all right. He's such a nice boy."

"Thank you, Maudie," Janet said to the young maid who placed platters of fried chicken and potatoes in front of them. The girl's eyes were red and she was barely controlling her tears.

Voices could be heard occasionally from the dining room, though Emma couldn't make out anything that was being said. She cut up a piece of chicken for Liam to pick at as Deelie attended to Orla, who was fussing.

"I hadn't met any of the brothers, except Andrew, but I think I saw them all today," Emma said. "I'm not sure how successful I'd be at telling them apart later, though. They look very much alike, don't they?" Not that she expected to have much contact with the family after what had happened. They wouldn't be in the mood to socialise. But her mother and grandmother would be asking questions when she got back to Wirramilla. Tragedies were always well talked over and the fallout possibilities dissected.

"They do that," Janet agreed around a mouthful of potato. "Evan and Harold are both clean shaven, if that helps you tell them from Frank and Declan. Ian just has a little wispy bit of fair hair on his chin, as you probably noticed. The others are all dark."

"Frank seemed to take Andrew's death particularly hard, I noticed."

Janet nodded. "He idolised Andrew."

At that moment, Frank's raised voice reached them, angry as if disagreeing with someone. "It weren't no accident. Andy was too careful, for that. And we know someone who wouldn't be unhappy to see Jack Brighten dead, don't we?"

Deelie looked up sharply, the colour draining from her face.

"It's bad enough what's happened without throwing accusations like that about. You need to calm down," another voice responded.

"What do you think the man did, Frank? Throw a lighted match into the mill? Don't be ridiculous," someone else put in.

"Lighted match." This said with scorn. "You know how easy it is to sabotage the place. Look at how Andy..."

Naomi closed the dining room door, shutting in the voices. She looked down the table to the three of them before seating herself again and attending to her meal. Emma saw Ann throw a glance their way as well.

"They think Bren did this," Deelie whispered. "Oh, Emma. I was just beginning to breathe again."

Emma, wondering at her friend's comment, reached out and gave her hand a comforting squeeze. Did this have anything to do with Brendan's run-in with the miller?

"It was an accident," Emma said. "You heard them. Frank is just upset." She noticed Janet wasn't saying anything.

Chapter 7

Deelie Confesses

EMMA LET DEELIE sleep after feeding Orla. Liam woke after a short nap, but it was too wet to go outside. She let him play in front of the kitchen fire. It would have been nice and cosy watching him, if she hadn't been concerned about the accident and what she had heard.

If Brendan were being accused of killing the miller – and by association, Andrew Lockwood – she wanted to know why. By the time Deelie woke, Emma had the table set out for afternoon tea, and had even managed to bake.

"Something smells delicious," Deelie said, when she came out of the bedroom. "I could get used to this."

"Fruit scones. They aren't as good as the one's you make, but they are edible at least. Liam says so, anyway." Emma indicated the little boy who was sitting at the table with a pillow under him, his head just above the tabletop. He gave his mother a cheeky grin.

"Well, aren't you just too smart, sitting up there," Deelie said.

Liam giggled and bit into his scone. Emma poured tea, and they sat.

"So, Deelie talk to me," Emma said, leaning forward and taking her friend's hand. "What is going on here?" Deelie stared down at her cup and didn't say anything. "I know something has been going on. Brendan and Jack Brighten were having an argument when I arrived. What was the trouble between them that would cause Frank Lockwood to accuse Brendan of sabotaging the mill to harm the man? That is what Frank was doing, wasn't it? Talk to me, please."

"It's all my fault," Deelie whispered tears in her voice.

"How is that?"

"Jack Brighten found out Bren and me only got married five months ago."

"Why would that matter to him?"

"He started saying things to Bren about me being a fallen woman, calling me nasty names, that I'd trapped him, how was Bren sure Orla was his. Things like that."

Emma gasped. "Oh, Deelie. I'm so sorry." She rubbed the girl's arm. "What a miserable man. But it isn't your fault."

"But it is. It was wrong of me I know, but I loved him. I loved Bren, and he was so sad after Bridget died. I couldn't bear to see him so sad and lonely. I just had to comfort him. And then... Oh," she drew in a trembling breath. "I'm being punished now. I was glad that man was dead. That's wicked too, isn't it? I shouldn't think things like that." She put her head down on her arms. Her voice was muffled with tears but Emma bending over her heard well enough. "Bren will lose his job, and no one will give him work if they think he killed Andrew Lockwood. He'll be hanged. What will become of us?"

Emma got up and put her arms around Deelie as she sat there. What strain had she been under these last few months? A new place, strange people, the birth of her first child. She hoped the girl wasn't suffering any depression after the birth. She was aware that with Deelie's background came strong religious feelings. Everything seemed to be all right between her and Brendan at least. She hoped there wasn't anything going on beneath the public face. Did Brendan think Deelie had trapped him into marriage? It didn't appear that way from what little she had seen to date, but who knew?

"Deelie, sweetheart. You're making too much of this. It's been a shock for everyone. It was completely unexpected. Everyone's upset. Come now. Where's the smart, brave girl I used to know?"

"I wish I was back home," Deelie cried, sitting up and brushing her hand across her eyes. "This isn't how it was supposed to be when me and Grainne set out. This was supposed to give us a better life. Now Grainne's gone, and I've made a mess of everything."

"Have you told Brendan how you feel?"

Deelie sniffed. "No. He'd be upset if I told him I didn't want to be here. You see how much he likes it. He's so pleased to learn to read and all."

Emma hesitated. Who was she to give marriage advice? Her marriage to Sam hadn't been one of great communication. Liam let out a cry and Emma managed to grab him before he fell off his chair, as the pillow he was sitting on slipped. She sat down again beside Deelie with Liam on her lap.

"I think you're feeling homesick," she said. "It's perfectly natural. You want your mother and sisters to be here to share your daughter, to help you the way they would if you were back in Ireland. You need to give things time to settle down, now."

"I do miss them so."

"Of course, you do. But you need to stop thinking you're being punished because you've done nothing wrong. Understand?" She squeezed Deelie's hand to emphasise the point. "You've just been a kind human being and you've got a lovely little girl and devoted husband to show for it. The only tragedy here is that the Lockwoods have lost Andrew."

"He accused Bren of trying to kill him."

"Who? Andrew?"

"No, *that man*. Bren told me last night. That's what they were arguing about. There was a fire in the mill the other morning and he blamed Bren. Said Bren put the nail between the millstones."

No surprise, then, where Frank Lockwood had got his idea from.

"Did Brendan ever work in the mill?"

"Once or twice. But not lately. Andrew stopped putting him there when he saw how things were. Bren said Jack Brighten didn't like the Irish and that's why he was picking on us. It's always been like that, Bren said. The English think the Irish aren't worth anything."

Emma knew Brendan's feelings about the English and their role in the Irish potato famine. He wasn't wrong about the English attitude, though. Anthony Trollope's Irish novels were not well received. The English weren't interested in Irish lives.

Deelie looked at her imploringly. "It was an accident. Wasn't it?" she asked.

"I can't see how it could be anything else," Emma assured her. She wasn't sure how you proved it, though.

JANET AND Rory joined them for supper, Janet bearing a hot casserole and Rory carrying an extra chair as lightly as if it were a teacup. During the afternoon, he and Brendan had been involved in making up the coffins, while the brothers retrieved the bodies from the wrecked mill once it was cool enough. Burial would take place in the morning. It was a subdued group that sat at the table, gathering for comfort rather than an enjoyable social meal.

"Does anyone know how Ian is faring?" Emma asked, as everyone filled their plates.

"Mrs. Fowler told me the doctor had him sedated," Janet reported. "Wants to keep him asleep for a day or so, apparently. Let his brain rest. Concussion, he said."

"I hope he'll be all right," Deelie said. "The family doesn't need to lose another of their own."

Everyone murmured agreement to that.

"We heard a little at lunch, about Frank's opinion. Has anything more been said?" Emma asked tentatively.

"Whatever happened, it had nothing to do with me," Brendan declared, his voice louder than normal. "But I can't pretend to be sorry that Jack Brighten is dead, God forgive me. He was making our lives a misery. Everyone heard the things he was saying about my wife."

Emma could see from the look Deelie gave him what the words 'my wife' meant to her. Janet and Rory both looked a little uncomfortable. Orla had been conceived out of wedlock after all, even if her parents were married now.

Rory cleared his throat. "Brighten was a bully. It's Andy they're grieving for, don't fret yourself on that score. Frank thought the sun rose and set on Andy. His head's full of rubbish right now." That seemed to cover Rory's opinion of Frank's claims, anyway. She found herself warming to the big Scotsman.

"He was well liked, then?" she asked. "Andrew, I mean. I only spoke to him once. He seemed – well – cold."

"You're not suggesting Andrew was the target if someone did this deliberately?" Janet looked at her sharply. "I wouldn't let anyone in the family hear you say that. That'll not be a popular idea."

"Well, Bren didn't do it to get rid of that man, that's for sure," Deelie said showing more spirit than Emma had seen since she arrived.

Rory tapped the table with his palm. "Hush, lassies. Don't get yourselves in a twist. It was an accident, nary a care what Frank Lockwood says."

Emma thought it wouldn't hurt to identify others with a motive to get rid of either the miller or Andrew Lockwood if Brendan were going to be accused.

"I just wondered what the situation was between the brothers, that's all. I mean, there are six of them." She paused. Were six. "They can't possibly agree on everything."

Janet shook her head, as if thinking Emma wasn't wise to pursue the matter. It didn't seem to bother Rory.

"There was friction between the boys," he admitted. "Andy could only expand so fast. Not everyone was patient with that."

Emma recalled the snippet of conversation she had heard in the barn.

"Andrew mentioned Evan's vineyard," she said. "I saw it when he was showing me over the mill." She shuddered at the thought of having been there such a short time ago. "Perhaps Evan wants to marry but he can't until there's more income and he thinks his vineyard could provide it. I mean, can you imagine six families living here with a couple dozen children? They'd need more than a few sheep and a flour mill to keep all those hungry mouths fed and bodies clothed."

"It's not the most sensible arrangement," Janet said, "but the Missus likes her boys around. I imagine some of them will move away in time."

"They would have to. This place can't possibly support all those people." Emma paused as she sopped up her gravy with a piece of bread. "This is delicious, by the way."

"It's just a beef stew but done the Scots way."

"It's the currant jelly makes the difference," Deelie put in.

"I'll have to remember that."

"Aye," Janet went on. "And they'd need more than once through the alphabet if all the boys married and lived here."

"The alphabet?" What was Janet talking about?

"Deelie hasn't told you about the family naming rules, then?"

"They have naming rules?"

"They do. They follow the alphabet, starting with Andrew and ending with O for Ophelia, up to now anyway. It was Mr. Xavier's idea, the Missus' late husband."

"That's the most bizarre thing I've ever heard," Emma said. "I suppose it makes it easy to see where everyone fits in."

"Well, it would do, if you knew your alphabet," Deelie muttered.

"So, Barbara must come after Andrew..."

"Aye," said Janet. "Six lads and three lasses there were." She counted them off on her fingers. "Andrew, Barbara, Clarissa – she's married and away – Declan, Evan, Frank, Georgia – Frank's twin, no longer with us, rest her soul – Harold and Ian. Then come the little ones. Katherine, Margaret, and baby Ophelia belong to Ruth and Andrew. Naomi and Declan have Jonathan, Laura, and wee Norman."

"I see. But wouldn't it have made more sense to start at the beginning again with the children?"

"No one said it had to make sense, hen."

At least they hadn't done the same with the dogs. Or had they? Perhaps Alfie was the first of Beauty's litter. Emma chided herself at the silly thought.

"Did you know Mr. Lockwood?" she asked. "I don't know how long you've been here yourselves."

"He was already poorly when we arrived. Five years ago, it must be now, eh Rory?"

"Aye, about that."

Emma wondered if Brendan and Deelie would be here in five years as she helped Deelie clear away the empty plates and serve the apple crumble they had made for dessert.

"Andrew said it was a nail between the millstones that caused the fire a few days ago," Emma said when she sat down at the table again. Janet sighed as if she'd had enough of the subject, but Brendan took it up.

"It only takes a little spark to ignite flour dust. It's always in the air in the mill. If the exhaust box is full and that catches, it could explode. It must have happened that way."

"You never told me the mill could explode when you were working there," Deelie said her tone indicating her dismay.

"I have to do what work I'm told. Worrying about it doesn't help."

Deelie frowned into her dessert.

"It was likely just the machinery being worn. Friction and heat," Rory put in.

"So, the mill was old?" Emma asked.

"It was built about ten, twelve years ago, I believe. Not old in terms of mills, but the machinery was secondhand." Which meant it may have been worn, causing friction.

The Fellings left shortly after finishing their meal, and Brendan and Deelie soon took themselves off to their room, further conversation not being desired. Emma was last out to the washhouse to wash and brush her teeth for bed.

As she rounded the corner to the outhouse, she saw the shadow of a man at the back door of Ruth's cottage taking his leave. One of the brothers checking on their grieving sister-in-law. Nothing odd in that. But why the back door?

Curious to see who it might be Emma hurried to the front in time to see someone come out from between the first two cottages, heading toward the back door of the homestead. Not Declan then, unless he wasn't intent on going to bed just yet. As he passed through the lamplight at the back verandah, she saw he was clean shaven. Evan or Harold, she couldn't be sure which. Did one of Andrew's younger brothers have an interest in his wife?

Chapter 8

Emma Interferes

EMMA WOKE EARLY again next morning. The sun was just appearing, and she could make out the shapes of trees and bushes in the backyard. The rain had passed. She heard Orla give a cry and Liam turned in his bed at the sound but didn't wake. Deelie would feed Orla before she and Brendan got up.

She dressed quickly. She was missing her daily walk by the river. There was a light in the window of Naomi's cottage as she passed, but Ruth's was still dark. No man getting up early for work there.

She went quietly out the gate to the side garden making sure Alfie wasn't nearby. As she reached the front of the homestead, she was startled to see a figure moving about the ruined mill with a flare held high. Was someone trying to find evidence that the mill had been sabotaged? Or were they looking to remove and hide such evidence if it existed?

The figure turned and by the light of the flare she recognised Frank Lockwood. He turned over some debris with a stick, bending low as he peered around. She moved up the rise, a wet, smoky smell greeting her as she got closer to the mill.

"Good morning. Are you looking for something?" she asked.

Frank started at the sound of her voice. "Who are you?"

"Emma Berry. I'm visiting the O'Neills." Perhaps not the best name to mention right now. She rushed on. "I'm sorry for your loss. I know what it's like to lose a brother."

Frank stared at her for a moment. He looked haggard and raw.

"Of course. I'd forgotten. You were on the bucket chain. I suppose I should thank you for helping."

The sun rose a little higher, brightening the site. It wasn't an improvement. The twisted machinery towered gauntly over what little was left of the shattered mill and scattered debris, like some monster from Emma's worst nightmare.

"It was the least I could do. What are you looking for?" Emma asked again as she casually took a few steps picking her way among the blackened shards.

"I'll know when I find it," Frank replied enigmatically.

Emma decided to push a little. "I heard that you suspect this wasn't an accident. Couldn't the explosion have been caused by a spark from the machinery, some friction?" She was repeating what Brendan and Rory had said. It seemed the logical explanation.

"No! No," he said again, more quietly but just as firmly. "There was a spark two days ago that caused a small fire. If it had been a spark yesterday it would have done the same. Andy would have put it out. He had buckets of water. He was careful, Andy was."

Emma didn't think there was much logic to that. It would all depend on where the spark originated in location to a sufficiently high concentration of flour dust.

"So, what do you think happened?"

"There was a flame. Someone introduced a flame. It had to be that."

"Did someone light a cigarette?"

"A cigarette?" He stared at her. "Of course not. That's ridiculous."

Emma couldn't imagine either the miller or Andrew being so careless in that regard either, but that was how accidents happened wasn't it? People being careless?

"How do you suppose it happened then, if not by accident?"

"I don't know. That's what I'm trying to figure out."

"Someone would have had to get close. Wouldn't they have been seen?" Perhaps Ian had seen something, but she remembered he was being kept sedated. Could he have been responsible? Could it have been a delayed fuse of some sort? She was woefully ill-informed on such matters.

Emma swept her gaze across the surroundings. The mill was located on a rise on open ground, with the partly built brick mill on the far side, the barn on the closer side, and the garden and homestead behind. About ten feet away, in the direction she was facing, was the bank of the dry billabong, and below that the river itself. Red gums populated the lower level on the far side of the billabong. Emma couldn't see how anyone would have been able to get close enough to the mill unseen.

"Well they weren't seen, were they?" Frank said. "Unless someone is keeping quiet about it. But I have my suspicions." Emma already knew what they involved.

Frank continued to scour the site, meticulously turning over each piece of timber and anything else that littered the area. He had just lost a brother, and he may not have wanted to talk to her, but she needed to put her case for Brendan. She didn't know if she would get another opportunity.

"I heard you accuse Brendan O'Neill of doing this to get back at the miller. Brendan might have fought the man, but it doesn't make sense that he would set the mill on fire and risk killing others as well. A person would have to be mad to do something like that."

That got Frank's attention. "You would say that, wouldn't you, being a friend. One would expect that. But he's Irish, isn't he? Who knows how he thinks?"

"The Irish are no madder than anyone else," Emma replied, trying to keep a quaver of concern from her voice.

"No? What about the Fenians? I've read about them in the papers. Exploding bombs in England, wrecking houses, killing innocent people. Everyone knows the Irish are mad." His voice was harsh with anger and pain, his eyes as cold as Andrew's had been.

Emma's hand went to her throat. The event in England he referred to had taken place almost ten years ago, but just this week the stories had been resurrected in people's minds with newspaper reports of Irish Fenian prisoners escaping in Fremantle. How safe were Brendan and Deelie, and the children, with suspicions like this in people's minds?

"Brendan isn't a Fenian. He's just a man trying to take care of his family."

"So you say. He might be here to stir up trouble for all I know. Why didn't he stay back at his previous place, eh? Why did he leave there?"

"There was no accommodation for a married man at Merrim Station." Well, that was partly the truth anyway.

"Huh." Frank turned and headed further into the ruin. Emma could smell the yeasty scent of cooked wheat.

"Anyway," he spun back to her, his face distorted, fury and grief mixed, "what about you? What did Andy have to say to you yesterday? Funny how this happens just after you turn up."

Emma stared, appalled. There was no point in responding. Frank Lockwood wasn't thinking clearly. Andrew Lockwood had talked to her about riverboats. It would have made more sense if he'd killed her, he'd seemed so keen to get his hands on one. Frank nodded at her a few times, as if to say, 'think on that,' before moving further away and going on with his search.

Emma hurried away. Her walk along the river would wait. She had to warn Brendan. Perhaps she should speak to Mrs. Lockwood as well. If Frank did find some evidence of sabotage – or thought he had – she didn't know how the rest of the family would react. The O'Neills might need protection.

"He accused me of being a Fenian, you say?" Brendan repeated, when Emma had poured out her conversation with Frank. He was sitting with a cup of tea, an empty plate attesting to his having eaten breakfast. She didn't bother to tell him Frank had accused her as well.

Deelie, sitting at the table with him, looked from her husband to Emma her face ashen. "What will they do? We should leave. How can we leave?"

"Wheest, girl, they won't do anything," Brendan assured her though the frown on his face belied his words. "He won't find anything to support his idea this was done on purpose, now."

"What if he does find something?" Deelie asked. "What if someone did make the explosion happen? They'll blame you."

"I'm going to speak with Mrs. Lockwood," Emma said. "I'll make sure she is aware of what Frank is doing."

"And Rory," Deelie said. "Tell Rory."

"I'll speak with Rory," Brendan said.

"What is Declan like? Would the others listen to him if Frank stirs them up?" Emma hadn't seen anything of Andrew's successor to judge.

"Declan's all right." Brendan said.

"I'll suggest Mrs. Lockwood talk to him." She'd speak to Declan herself, but it would be forward of her to interfere to that extent.

"The man isn't thinking clearly, for sure," Brendan said, shaking his head. "The Fenians aren't for working on a farm. They're for inciting riots and the like."

"I'll tell her that."

"Be careful," breathed Deelie, clinging to Brendan as he kissed her cheek before leaving for work. She sat staring at the door after it had closed behind him as if willing him to reappear. Emma hoped she wasn't making too much of Frank's words and frightening everyone unnecessarily. But to not say anything and have something happen – that would be far worse.

<><><>

EMMA FOUND Barbara and Mrs. Fowler in the kitchen elbows deep in cake batter and scone dough at the large, scrubbed pine table. Two of the maids, one of them Maudie, were at the sink cleaning up after the family's breakfast. The kitchen was large and warm, the fireplace dominating the space. It was fitted with a large double door oven putting the kitchen at Wirramilla to shame. But then the Lockwood family was much larger.

"Good morning," she said. "I'm sorry to bother you at this time but I'm looking for Mrs. Lockwood. Would I be able to talk to her? It's rather important."

Barbara looked at her quizzically. "She's with Ian." Barbara's eyes were red, and she looked tired.

"How is he doing?"

"Still sleeping. Doc Wilson will be back this afternoon to see him."

"Along with a host of people to pay their respects," Mrs. Fowler put in, whisking eggs into her cake batter. "We're going to be baking all morning. Nothing like a wake to sharpen people's appetites."

"Really, Mrs. Fowler," Barbara remonstrated.

"Sorry, dear. But it's the truth none the less. As if people being reminded their time is short on this earth feel they need to enjoy their lot while they still can."

Barbara glanced back at Emma and raised her eyebrows, as if to say, 'what can you do?'

Emma held back a smile. "Please accept my condolences, Barbara," she said instead. "I know what it is to lose a brother." It was the second time that morning she had said it. "My older brother, Michael, died in a riding accident when he was twelve."

Barbara pushed a strand of hair from her forehead with her wrist to avoid getting dough on her face, unsuccessfully as it turned out.

"Thank you. Andy's going to leave a big space in our lives, I'm afraid." Her voice wobbled. "Anyway, Ma will be along shortly. Unless I can help you?"

"Thank you, but I would rather speak to your mother, if you don't mind."

Barbara shrugged, looking as if she would love to know what it was about. Did she think Emma was going to tell them Brendan had caused the mill explosion?

Mrs. Fowler bustled two cake tins into one of the ovens and started adding herbs and spices to a bowl of minced meat.

"Can I help with anything in the meantime?" Emma offered.

"Here." Mrs. Fowler sprinkled flour on a spare section of the table and slapped down a lump of flaky pastry she retrieved from a bowl on the sideboard.

"You can roll this out for me. Long and narrow for the beef rolls."

Emma took off her jacket and hung it over the back of a chair before rolling up the sleeves of her blouse. She took up the rolling pin and began to roll out the dough. She thought of Deelie worrying at home alone. There was nothing she could do to speed up what she had set herself to do. Her head began to ache as she thought how to word what she needed to say to Mrs. Lockwood without directly criticising Frank.

"How is your grandmother doing?" Mrs. Fowler asked after a few minutes of relative quiet.

"Keeping well, and busy as always," Emma said.

She wasn't surprised at the question. Everyone along the rivers knew of her grandmother and her herbal remedies. Barbara pulled a tray of golden scones from the smaller of the two ovens.

"Are you going to take over her work?" she asked.

Was she? She wasn't sure what the future held for her yet. If she remained single and continued to live at Wirramilla she supposed she would eventually. When she stopped travelling on the *Mary B* anyway.

She was prevented from answering by the appearance of Mrs. Lockwood. Barbara and Mrs. Fowler immediately wanted to know how Ian was doing and were told he was still sleeping. Emma noticed how tired and drawn the woman looked. Barbara obviously did as well, as she gave her mother a hug leaving floury handprints on her clothes, something neither of them seemed to be concerned about.

"This is very thoughtful of you, Mrs. Berry, to help out," she said.

"Emma, please. It's the least I can do."

"Ma, Emma wants to talk to you. Why don't you have a cup of tea and sit out in the vestibule."

Barbara ushered them both out, leaving them with the tea tray and a few hot scones.

"I haven't had a chance to say how dreadfully sorry I am for your loss," Emma told the older woman when they were seated.

"Thank you," Mrs. Lockwood said simply.

Emma took a breath and continued as gently as possible.

"I saw Mr. Frank searching among the mill ruins this morning. He's terribly upset, which is perfectly understandable, but… I'm just a little concerned. He seems determined to find proof that the explosion was deliberately caused by someone. He was…" she was about to say raving, but caught herself in time, "talking of Irish Fenians, and how they are bent on causing death and mayhem.

"Just because Brendan is Irish doesn't make him a Fenian, Mrs. Lockwood. Brendan's just a hard-working man like everyone else here. He has no connection with the Fenians, and he isn't a violent man. I've known him long enough to know that. I'm sorry to worry you, I just thought you should know, to stop it before it goes any further."

Mrs. Lockwood looked at Emma squarely, silent for a moment. Emma wished she could tell what the woman was thinking.

"Declan told me what Frank said at lunch yesterday," Mrs. Lockwood said. "He is upset. We all are. The idea of someone doing such a thing deliberately..." She shook her head. "But we all know Jack Brighten and Brendan O'Neill didn't get along, for whatever reason. It's not unexpected that people might see more to the matter."

Was Frank not the only one? Mrs. Lockwood certainly didn't seem to be against the possibility.

"I can't imagine how anyone could have done it deliberately," Emma said. "No one could have approached the mill without someone seeing them, and they would have been caught in the explosion themselves." As Ian was, she suddenly thought, and hurried on. "It had to have been an accident. I'm just concerned that accusations could turn into action without any proof."

"We are not a lynch mob, Mrs. Berry," she said stiffly.

"Of course not." She wasn't making a particularly good job of this. "I just thought you should be aware of what is being said. Forewarned is always best, wouldn't you say?" Mrs. Lockwood shook her head. The conversation was now officially awkward. Emma stood, abandoning her barely tasted cup of tea. "Thank you for listening to me."

Had she made matters worse, making more of Frank's rant than necessary? But she was concerned. Rumours could spread and follow Brendan for the rest of his life.

"There will be a wake this afternoon," Mrs. Lockwood announced as Emma turned away. "I expect everyone to be here to pay their respects. But I won't have talk and speculation on what has happened among our friends and neighbours."

"Of course not," Emma said, turning back to her. "Thank you for the invitation." More like an order. Mrs. Lockwood might be better advised to tell Frank not to attend. He was the one likely to stir up talk.

Chapter 9

The Wake

EMMA AND THE O'Neills might have felt obliged to attend the wake for Andrew Lockwood but they weren't in any hurry to do so. Waiting until most of the guests had arrived in the hope of blending in unnoticed felt like the better option.

Deelie deposited Liam in the vestibule where the maid Maudie and Ann Russell were taking care of the youngest Lockwood children and several young visitors. Ann looked as if she wanted to follow them to the dining room. Emma felt a pang of sympathy for her. She was reminded of the way Barbara had spoken to Ann yesterday. The schoolteacher appeared to be treated more as a servant than the professional she was.

There was a queue of people in the drawing room, waiting to pay their condolences to the family. Some stood alone while others formed small groups, speaking quietly. Mrs. Lockwood, Barbara, Naomi and Ruth, all in black, were seated together on a sofa on the far side of the room, the boys standing behind as friends and neighbours sat briefly in the nearby arm-chairs to speak to them.

Emma was greeted with nods of recognition from several people as she and the O'Neills joined the queue. As they moved closer Emma saw that Ruth Lockwood's outfit had been patchily dyed and was at least a size too small. Perhaps it had shrunk during the hasty dyeing process. Evan was hovering behind her his hand on the back of the sofa by her shoulder.

Tom Gulbis was standing between Evan and Declan. Frank was glaring at everyone without fa-vouritism. His face darkened further at seeing Brendan when their turn came but he said nothing. They didn't sit but offered some carefully chosen words and then quickly and quietly disappeared into the dining room where food was set out on the table and they were as far from the family as possible.

Emma breathed a sigh of relief. The worst was over. At the table, Deelie had her hands full with Orla so Brendan put some food for her on his plate along with a slice of beef roll for himself. Emma chose a slice of cake and two little pastry tarts. They moved back from the table to allow others access.

A portrait above the fireplace, framed in an ornate gold-coloured surround, caught Emma's eye and she drew in a sharp breath. The subject was a severe look-ing man with the long face that seemed typical of the Lockwood men. He was sitting very upright, hair brushed back from his face, a neatly trimmed pointed beard. But it was his eyes, a deep blue-grey, that caught her attention. Just like Andrew's. They seemed to be looking straight at her and not in a friendly way.

"Deelie, is that a portrait of Mrs. Lockwood's husband?" she asked.

Deelie followed Emma's gaze. "It is. That's Mr. Xavier. Ian painted it."

"Such a gentleman, dear Xavier," a woman standing nearby said, enunciating her vowels clearly. "He would be absolutely devastated at this tragedy."

Emma turned to see Mrs. Wilson, the wife of their local doctor.

"I'm sure any parent would be, Mrs. Wilson," she agreed. "May I introduce my friends, Brendan and Deelie O'Neill. I'm visiting with them for the week."

"How nice," Mrs. Wilson said barely glancing at them. "I was wondering how you had got here so quickly. Yes, such a dreadful thing to lose a child. And how brave dear Isabel is. I would be prostrate if anything happened to my dear Zoe."

Emma nodded to Miss Zoe Wilson who was standing beside her mother, a replica of her female parent with her nose always raised a little higher than was polite.

"You know the family well?" Emma asked, irritated but not surprised at Mrs. Wilson's dismissal of her Irish friends.

"We have been dear friends for years. I'm sure in due course we will be even closer," she simpered, glancing sideways at Zoe who lowered her gaze modestly.

"Oh? So, congratulations are in order? Who is the lucky man?"

"Well, nothing has been declared yet, you understand," Mrs. Wilson hastened to say, "but between you and me, Mrs. Berry, Mr. Evan is truly smitten. It is only a matter of time."

How interesting. Evan Lockwood seemed to be in some demand. She must meet this man who was smitten with Zoe Wilson and secretly visiting his newly widowed sister-in-law. She was sure it was Evan who had left Ruth's cottage on the evening of the explosion. Seeing the brothers standing together just now had confirmed Evan of being a lighter build than Harold and a good inch taller.

A sixteen-year-old girl moved into Emma's view from beside Zoe Wilson. She wore her hair tied back with a ribbon, and a grey dress that was far too old for her. It wasn't enough to hide the pretty fresh face of Dr. Wilson's niece and ward, however much Mrs. Wilson might try to keep her from outshining her daughter.

"Lizzie, how are you?" Emma greeted her with a smile.

"Very well, thank you, Mrs. Berry," Lizzie Ballard replied politely.

Mrs. Wilson shot a quick glance at the girl and Lizzie slipped back out of view, but not before Emma caught the flash of an impish grin. Good for her.

"And how is your dear grandmother?" Mrs. Wilson purred. "Still making up her little remedies?" Belittle them she may but her husband was one of their best customers and she was certain Mrs. Wilson made use of them when she needed. "And yourself, dear? I must say, I wouldn't like my daughter living on a riverboat. Not quite – well, you know – for a young lady."

"It's an exciting life, Mrs. Wilson. I wouldn't change it for anything," Emma told her. "And it is a family affair after all."

"Well..."

"Mrs. Berry. I didn't expect to see you here."

"Lieutenant Forrester." Emma greeted him more warmly than she may have done had Mrs. Wilson not been listening. Give her something more to gossip about. The man was a head taller than her, stiff in his military bearing, moustache bristling. She wasn't sure if he was pleased to see her or not. The latter most likely. "Are you a friend of the family?" she asked, wondering how he could have gotten here from Euston in the time.

"No, I'm here in an official capacity. I've been seconded to Wentworth for six months. Captain Lockhart is visiting family back Home." Home being

England, of course. Emma could almost hear the capital letter.

"You are investigating these deaths?" Emma asked sharply. Had the Lockwoods called him in? Were they treating this as murder after all?

Lieutenant Forrester's eyebrows rose at her tone. "Every death has to be investigated, Mrs. Berry, even when it's accidental. There will be an inquest, of course. Accidents are not uncommon in the flour milling industry. Tragic in this case with the loss of a man from a prominent local family and with a young family of his own. It's a volatile business."

Emma relaxed a little. "It is indeed." She looked around and realised that Brendan and Deelie had disappeared. Well, she couldn't blame them. Janet Felling appeared at her side and Emma introduced her to the Lieutenant.

"Lovely turn out," Janet said. "I think all of Wentworth's who's who and some that aren't are here. Just to see and be seen most of them, too. Have you seen all the casseroles and roast meats the good ladies of the district have brought? Mrs. Fowler will be able to take the week off."

Emma was surprised at Janet's tone. But then the Scots and the Irish saw a wake as a celebration of a life. And she had no idea what Janet's personal feelings were toward Andrew or Jack Brighten. Or what anyone else present felt for that matter. The conversation in the room was muted as befitting the occasion, but seemed to be more a case of respect, and perhaps shock, than any great sense of grief.

"But how anyone is expected to balance a plate of food and a cup of tea and actually eat and drink I will never understand," Janet went on.

"I know I need a cup of tea," Emma said. "I would love to wash down some of this cake, but there's no side table to put the plate on for a few minutes."

"Let me hold it for you, Mrs. Berry," Lieutenant Forrester offered. "I will be your side table."

Emma looked at the Lieutenant in surprise. Why was he being so amenable? Or was this how he normally behaved when he wasn't investigating a murder that she was involved with? He seemed to think these deaths had been accidental. She hoped nothing would occur to change that opinion.

"Why, thank you. That's most thoughtful of you."

He took the plate in his gloved hand. He really was rather handsome, she had to admit. Janet gave her a sly sideways glance.

"I'll get the tea, hen. You stay here and keep the Lieutenant company." She disappeared into the dining room as Emma stifled a sigh.

Why did everyone think she wanted to be roman-tically linked with every gentleman she spoke to? The dining room was becoming increasingly crowded and they found themselves shuffled back toward the corner. At least from there she couldn't see the por-trait of Xavier Lockwood, though she could still feel his eyes seeking her out. Lieutenant Forrester was standing a little closer than she thought he needed to, but she had to be able to reach her plate she supposed. She took a bite out of one of the fruit tarts.

"Have you known the Lockwood family long, Mrs. Berry," the Lieutenant asked quietly, leaning his head in closer as he spoke.

"I don't really know them at all, in fact," she replied in like tone. "I met Mrs. Lockwood some months ago quite by accident, and when my friends Deelie and Brendan O'Neill were looking for a new place I asked Mrs. Lockwood if she had a position. They ended up here back in November. The only other members of the Lockwood family I have spoken to were Andrew himself, and Barbara and Frank. I doubt the other brothers even know who I am."

"Oh, I doubt that Mrs. Berry. I doubt that very much. You must know you are a legend in your own right along the river. For more reasons than one."

Emma stilled. More reasons than one? Was he referring to her position on a riverboat or her rumoured relationship with her brother-in-law? How bold of him.

"Am I indeed," she said her voice cool.

"I am referring to your daring-do, ma'am. There aren't many women who would drag a murderer into the river in order to achieve his capture." She was sure his moustache was twitching. And was that a twinkle in his eye?

"I believe you are laughing at me. That is hardly chivalrous, for all you are holding my plate for me."

He cleared his throat and became serious. "I apologise. It is hardly the occasion for levity. I was rather hoping you could give me some information on how things are situated at River Bend. Seeing as you are here after all." At least he hadn't come expecting to interview her. "I couldn't ask for a more unbiased informant."

If only he knew.

"Here you are." Janet appeared bearing two cups of tea and handed one to Emma. "I'll just take this one to Rory," she said, with a quick glance between Emma and the Lieutenant.

She was off again, edging her way through the gathering. Emma was sure the second cup had been meant for Janet herself.

"Have you spoken to the family?" she asked, taking a sip of tea.

"Apart from offering my condolences, no. I asked Declan Lockwood to give me some time later this afternoon."

"So, you want to see if my story of what happened matches his?"

"I was hoping for a little more background, but if you don't know the family well, I will take what I can get."

Emma nodded. "Do you know anything about the miller, Jack Brighten?" she asked, taking advantage of the situation to ask a question of her own. "Does he have any family in the colonies?" There were many who did not.

"It doesn't appear so. He only came out from England two years ago. I had a telegraph from Adelaide confirming his arrival there. He's worked in several mills in South Australia. A difficult man to get along with, it would appear." Emma nodded. That she could agree with. "His connections in England will be notified of his death, of course."

"Of course."

"Could we find somewhere else to talk, Mrs. Berry? This isn't the most perfect place for an interview, and I may need to take notes."

Emma only knew the public spaces in the homestead, and they were all occupied. She didn't want to take him to Deelie's cottage. That seemed like an intrusion on their hospitality.

"There's a bench seat out in the side garden. It should be quiet there."

She relieved the Lieutenant of her empty plate and he put his hand on her elbow as he guided them through the main throng. Emma was just depositing her cup and plate on a trolley put there the purpose when she felt a touch on her shoulder.

"I should have known you'd be in trouble with the police soon enough." Her brother grinned at her wickedly. "How are you, Lieutenant?"

"Joe! I'm nothing of the sort." She gave him a peck on the cheek.

"I'm very well, thank you Haythorne," Lieutenant Forrester nodded to him in a genial manner.

"The Lieutenant is asking for my help if you must know. Is Catherine here with you?"

"No. She didn't care to make the journey. Besides, she doesn't know the family personally, so my presence is enough."

Emma nodded. His own presence was simply a matter of politeness anyway.

"The Lieutenant and I were just going outside to talk. Why don't you join us?" she suggested. That should stop the tongues wagging anyway. Her brother was the perfect chaperone. Joe agreed and the Lieutenant made no objection.

The bench seat in the side garden was commod ious enough for the three of them, which was fortunate as Joe insisted on Emma sitting next to the Lieutenant, otherwise they would be talking across him.

"You could do worse," Joe whispered as he took his seat. Emma rubbed her ear, letting him know she wasn't interested in anything he had to say on that subject.

At the Lieutenant's prompting Emma described the events of the previous morning as the Lieutenant made notes.

"Then it started to rain, quite heavily, and the women left the rest of it to the men. I heard the bodies were retrieved later in the day and were to be buried this morning. I presume that was done."

"And you saw everyone there at the time?" he asked.

Emma's attention was distracted for a moment as Barbara and Ruth Lockwood appeared from the back of the homestead, making their way to Ruth's cottage. Here they were, discussing the deaths matter-of-factly when others were feeling as if their lives had been shattered forever. She knew what that was like. She would visit Ruth at some point and offer what comfort she could, although she couldn't say her first meeting with the woman had brought out any feelings of comradeship.

"Mrs. Berry?"

"Oh, sorry. What was the question again?"

"Everyone was there when all this was going on?"

"Oh, well I can't really say, as I don't know everyone who lives here. Besides, I was down the lower side of the billabong on the bucket line to begin with, so couldn't see much of what was happening up top."

"Very well. Name who you saw."

Naming the family members was simple enough. All she had to do was run through the alphabet as

Janet had done. Fortunately, she didn't have to name the children.

"Evan didn't answer his mother's roll call," she added, "but he was there later when the rain started. Then there was Mrs. Fowler, she's the housekeeper, the maids Gladys and Maudie, I don't know the name of the other one. Brendan and Deelie O'Neill, Janet and Rory Felling, he's the blacksmith, and Ann Russell the schoolteacher. Oh, and two men working on the new mill. One of them rode for Dr. Wilson to attend Ian Lockwood."

"A tragic accident," Joe murmured.

"One certainly hopes so," she said.

Lieutenant Forrester looked at her sharply. "You suspect it wasn't?"

"I don't suspect anything. But, well, you are bound to hear about it eventually. The problem is not everyone thinks it was an accident."

"Really? Who would that be and why?"

"Frank Lockwood was searching the ruins early this morning looking for evidence of sabotage. He thinks Brendan is involved. It's ridiculous of course. Just because he had an argument with the miller. Brendan wouldn't dream of doing such a thing, and anyway it was impossible. No one could have got close to the mill to cause an explosion, not without getting caught up in it themselves." She was reminded of Ian Lockwood once again. "And all Frank

Lockwood's talk about Fenians and the Irish is ridiculous. They wouldn't..."

"Whoa, hold on, now. One of the brothers is claiming the explosion of the mill was caused deliberately?"

"That's what I said."

Joe and the Lieutenant exchanged a look across her.

"How would they have done it?" Joe asked.

"That's the question, isn't it? No one can say."

At the Lieutenant's request for details, Emma told what she had heard at lunchtime when Frank first made his accusations, and Frank's diatribe at the mill site early that morning.

"And when I told Mrs. Lockwood about it, she got very defensive."

"As in trying to cover up what someone in the family might have done?" Lieutenant Forrester asked.

"Well, no. I was concerned about Brendan and Deelie. Mrs. Lockwood thought I was making much of little. They weren't a lynch mob, her words."

"But you said no one agreed with Frank when he made the claim at lunch yesterday."

"Not then, they didn't. But you know how easily that could change."

"That's a bit paranoid, isn't it?" put in Joe.

Was she being paranoid? Frank's attitude bothered her. Was it just his grief at Andrew's death? Or did he really have reason to believe the mill was sabotaged? And if it was, how and by whom?

The Lieutenant considered for a moment. "I will let the family know that I'm aware of the accusation. They're not likely to do anything silly. I don't know them, I must admit, but they are well respected in the district. I have no cause yet to station a man here or to remove the O'Neills for their own safety. I would suggest the man is just searching for an explanation where there isn't one."

Emma thought, once again, that the hardest thing would be to prove that it had been an accident. Unless you could do that, there could always be speculation.

After the Lieutenant had gone about his business, Emma and Joe went back into the homestead. Emma saw Tom Gulbis in the thinning crowd, talking to Dr. Wilson. He wouldn't have been expecting to come back so soon, especially not in support of one of his daughters who had become a widow.

Chapter 10

Frank Finds a Clue

SUNDAY WAS QUIET and uneventful. No work was done, and everyone kept to themselves. Emma hoped it wasn't the quiet before the storm. Naomi's two older children, Jonathan and Laura were playing outside. When Emma took Liam out to enjoy the sunshine and fresh air Alfie entertained them all, and himself, running around and generally getting in everyone's way.

At some point during the morning, Evan Lockwood came out onto the back verandah, looked about, hesitated, and went back in. Had he been going to visit Ruth again and decided not to because he had seen her seeing him? Emma couldn't imagine why it would matter, but he had seemed to change his mind after seeing her sitting there.

The mill site was a hive of activity next morning. Emma and Deelie, drawn by the noise, went to see what was being done. Rory and Brendan and several men Emma hadn't seen before were collecting up the loose scattered debris and loading it onto a flatbed wagon. The Lockwood brothers all seemed to be concentrating their attentions on the mill itself, hauling out the burnt timbers and chopping down those still standing.

Emma and Deelie joined Barbara, Mrs. Fowler and Naomi by the front door.

"Ma wants it out of sight as soon as possible," Barbara told them, as Deelie seated herself on the sofa with Orla. "She can't abide the sight of it."

Emma could understand the sentiment. "Where are they putting it all?"

"They're making a pile down past the horse paddock. They'll burn the timbers and bury whatever is left."

Out of sight, out of mind. Frank Lockwood appeared from behind the mill. He seemed to be looking carefully at and under everything he picked up. Apparently, he hadn't given up the idea of sabotage just yet. Declan shouted at him to stop wasting time and give a hand inside the mill. Frank ignored him. Emma crossed her fingers on the wish that clearing the site would be the end of it, once and for all.

"How is Ian?" Deelie asked.

"He's much better, thank you Deelie," Barbara replied. "He's awake and eating everything in sight. It's such a relief. I don't know what Ma would have done if she lost him too."

"That is such good news."

"I'm going to put the kettle on, if you are interested in a cuppa," Mrs. Fowler said to Deelie and Emma. "There's still plenty of food left over from Saturday. I'll be throwing it out in another day or so. Better it gets eaten. There's only so much stale cake we can make use of in trifles. It'll be beef and lamb casseroles for lunch today."

Emma helped Mrs. Fowler carry the tea things out to the vestibule as Deelie settled herself at the table with the children. Neither Barbara nor Naomi had followed them in. She didn't imagine they had any interest in having tea with the housekeeper. For Emma it was an opportunity to learn something.

"I see that policeman was having a good chat with you at the wake," Mrs. Fowler said. "Lucky your brother was there to chaperone, sitting out by yourselves."

Emma knew someone would have noticed. Mrs. Fowler was obviously curious about what had been said.

"I've met the Lieutenant before, when he was at Euston," Emma said. "He just wanted to know what had happened here and didn't want to bother the family with too many painful questions. I was just convenient. As was Joe."

Mrs. Fowler nodded sagely. "You told him about Mr. Frank accusing Deelie's man, though, didn't you?" Emma nodded. "Would have been better if you hadn't. There was a right to-do about that, later."

"I was afraid it might get out of hand, Mrs. Fowler. If anything happened to Brendan and I hadn't said anything I would never have forgiven myself. You wouldn't want any of the brothers charged with assaulting him, would you?"

"That's as may be," Mrs. Fowler said, looking only slightly appeased at the explanation.

"So, it caused some trouble?"

"Isabel, Mrs. Lockwood," she corrected herself, "told Frank she didn't want the police sticking their nose into family business. They never had any trouble with the law before and they weren't about to start now. Their father would be turning over in his grave, she said. Mr. Declan said much the same. Told Mr. Frank he would knock some sense into him if he didn't stop with that rot. It got right heated."

"How did Mr. Frank take it?"

"Not well. He still refuses to believe Mr. Andrew could be so careless, but he hasn't said anything since, that I've heard of anyway." She shook her head sadly.

Emma remembered her brother Michael, six years older and so good at everything, or so it had seemed to her young mind at the time. She felt for Frank's grief. It would be as if the sun had disappeared from his life. It had from her mother's when Michael died and never reappeared.

"You can't question God's will," Deelie, herself no stranger to grief, put in quietly.

"Amen to that," Mrs. Fowler said.

"No one seems to be grieving for Jack Brighten," Emma commented.

The kitchen door slammed. "You should come and see this," Barbara called. Emma's stomach clenched. Had Frank found something? She caught Deelie's eye, the alarm she felt echoed in her friend's face. "Declan is putting one of the broken millstones in the garden as a memorial," Barbara told them. "Come on. We can watch from the verandah."

Emma's stomach settled back into place. She reached out and squeezed Deelie's arm. Her friend gave her a wan smile. They would both be glad when this was over.

They trooped out through the kitchen to the partly closed-in side verandah. Ian was sitting at the far end in an open section that overlooked the garden. He was bundled in a blanket, looking pale, a bandage wrapping half his head. Mrs. Lockwood stood beside him. Out in the garden, the wagon had been backed up as close as possible to the path. Inside was a millstone with a large ragged gap on one side where a piece had been blown off in the explosion.

"Where are you going to put it?" Mrs. Lockwood wanted to know.

"Haven't decided," Declan Lockwood told her.

Emma studied him up close for the first time. Much like his older brother beard and all, but with a softer look about the eyes and mouth. There followed some discussion, with Barbara chipping in her thoughts until it was finally decided to put the mill-stone in the garden bed behind the bench seat, where Emma had sat with Joe and Lieutenant Forrester. Emma didn't think Mrs. Lockwood was all that pleased to have it anywhere but was giving in on this point at least to her now eldest son.

Evan and Harold began to dig a hole in which to stand the millstone. Brendan and Rory stood off to the side. The brothers apparently considered this was their job to deal with in honour of Andrew. Except she couldn't see Frank. Was he back at the mill still searching for the elusive evidence?

"Wait. Let me fetch the girls." Barbara hurried away to the cottages.

The maid Maudie appeared from within the home-stead, looking curious as to what was going on, and Mrs. Fowler sent her to fetch Ann Russell and the children from the schoolhouse. Barbara returned with Ruth and Naomi. Gladys and the third little maid carried the youngest two Lockwoods. They were joined a minute later by Ann and her charges. Ann gave Ruth a hug, which was received matter-of-factly while Naomi stood a little apart. Emma wondered again at the sister's relationship. She hadn't seen any interaction between them since she had been at River Bend.

The women watched in silence as the digging went on. Emma would have liked to leave but felt it would be rude to do so now she was here. Once the hole was deemed deep enough, Harold, Evan and Declan manhandled the millstone off the wagon, moving it – roll, thump, roll, thump – between the flower beds to its resting place. With some grunting and a softly spoken curse or two, the stone was manoeuvred into place damaged side down, the hole backfilled and the soil stomped down. The men stepped away to admire their handiwork. The millstone had been buried to a little more than half its depth. No one spoke for a minute or two.

"A job well done," Mrs. Fowler said eventually into the silence.

"You could grow something over to soften it, Ma," Barbara suggested, stepping down off the verandah and going to inspect the installation.

"Right. We've still some time before lunch," Declan said. "We can get..."

"I've found it! Here, I've found it." Frank came running, holding something up in his hand. "It was underneath the millstone. It was there all the time. That explosion wasn't an accident. It was done on purpose. I knew it. I knew it."

No one moved for several seconds. It was like a tableau, everyone turned to statues as they took in Frank's words. Then Deelie turned to Emma with a look of horror on her face. Someone screamed, Ann or Ruth perhaps. Mrs. Lockwood looked as though she was about to collapse.

Declan grabbed his brother's arm to see what he was holding.

"It's an arrowhead, Frank." His tone was dismissive.

"Look at it. An arrowhead with a burnt shaft and a tiny piece of stuff wired to it. It's a fire arrow. What is a fire arrow doing in the mill?"

A fire arrow? Were they serious? What did these people get up to?

Declan seemed to echo her thoughts. "Don't be ridiculous..."

But Evan and Harold had joined them.

"Frank's right. There's wire…" Evan said as he examined the arrowhead. Harold took it from him and held it up.

"Yeah, and a tiny piece of stuff, right here." He pointed it out. "You can just see it, stuck under where the ends of the wire are twisted together. It's almost burnt right off."

"It might have caused the explosion if someone shot it in through an opening," Evan said.

"Murderer," Frank shouted making a sudden dash for Brendan, trampling over a garden bed on the way. "You killed my brother."

Brendan, standing off to the side of the newly erected millstone, stood his ground as Frank rushed him but it was Rory who stepped forward and halted Frank with one hand, spinning him around. Frank lost his balance and Rory grabbed his arm, keeping him upright. Frank shook him off and turned back toward Brendan, but Rory was a solid wall before him.

"That's for the police to decide. It is, isn't it?" Rory said directing his words to Declan.

"Police. I don't think we need the police. We can work this out ourselves." Declan looked from Rory and Brendan to his brothers. No one seemed sure of the answer to that.

Then Brendan came forward, sidestepping Frank who looked as if he could commit murder himself right then.

"I had nothing to do with this," he told Declan clearly. "You need to look to your own."

He held out his hand and Deelie stepped off the verandah. He put his arm about her shoulder as they walked away to their cottage, every eye on them as they went. Rory stood hands on hips as if daring any-one to try anything untoward. The air crackled with tension. Emma, still holding Liam, was torn between going with the O'Neills or staying to hear what happened next. In her friends' interest she stayed.

"What did O'Neill mean, look to our own?" Harold growled. Liam whimpered, and Emma realised she was holding him tightly, her body tense. She relaxed her hold and soothed him. She didn't need attention drawn to her right now.

Declan took a step toward the verandah and his youngest brother.

"Ian, you were right there. What did you see?"

Ian straightened up slightly in his chair. "I can't remember anything about it."

"You must have seen something."

"Doc said his memory might be affected for a while," Barbara put in, moving back toward the verandah. "Don't bully him, Dec."

"How could someone shoot a fire arrow in the middle of the day and no one see anything? Which of you was out shooting?" Declan turned on Evan and Harold, accusing. "Come on. Out with it. Who was it?" The brothers looked at one another and back at Declan, shaking their heads. "None of us would have done it on purpose," Declan went on, wheedling for an answer. "It had to be a wild shot. An unlucky shot."

"Would it? What about you, Dec," Frank challenged, putting himself in his brother's face. "You had the most to gain from Andy's death. The place is yours now. You get to do whatever you want. You're already making changes. Hey? What about it?"

"I don't want anything I didn't already have, Frank." Declan's face was now inches from Frank's as they glared at one another.

"Take it easy," Evan said pulling his younger brother by the shoulder.

"And what about you?" Frank said, turning his attention to Evan. "Looks like you might get the money for your vineyard now Andy's not got his hands on the purse."

Evan blanched. "You're mad if you think I would kill him for that. I was going to get it anyway eventually For all we know, that arrow could have been lying about in the mill for months."

"Ev's right, Frank," Declan said, clutching at the idea like a drowning man clutching at a lifebuoy.

Frank's fists were clenched by his side. "I don't believe it. Someone shot a fire arrow into the mill. On purpose. To kill that miller or Andy. Doesn't matter which, the result was the same. Someone's going to pay for it. Someone's..."

"Stop. Stop right now." It was Mrs. Lockwood, in command of herself again except for the tremor in her voice. "Give me that arrowhead. Now, Declan," she ordered, raising her voice as he didn't move.

Barbara walked up to the combatants and snatched it from her brother's hand. Declan made to grab it back, but Barbara skipped away up to the verandah and handed the arrowhead to her mother. Mrs. Lockwood didn't even look as she closed her hands on it. If Barbara wanted thanks, she wasn't getting any.

"There will be no more accusations and threats," Mrs. Lockwood said. "Is that understood?" Her sons looked down, embarrassed either at accusing one another or at being admonished by their mother in front of everyone. "Is that clear?" Mrs. Lockwood waited for their nods and murmured agreement. "Now, if anyone has a confession to make about shooting arrows that morning, they need to tell me. Otherwise, the police will have to be called to get to the bottom of this."

"Ma..." Declan began to protest.

"The police," Mrs. Lockwood said, with a glance in Emma's direction. All eyes turned to her.

"Well?" Declan said. "If anyone has anything to say now is the time."

Evan, Harold, and Frank sent sideways looks at one another and back to Declan once again. No one was confessing to anything.

Mrs. Lockwood let out a heartfelt sigh, full of sadness and resignation. "Someone will have to ride into Wentworth and get hold of Lieutenant Forrester."

"I'll go," Harold said. He strode off, grim faced.

Frank nodded, satisfied. He didn't say anything but might as well have. 'Now, we'll see,' was the clear message.

Mrs. Fowler and Barbara, followed by Maudie, made their way to the kitchen past where Emma was standing. Maudie was the only one who glanced at her. As the garden and verandah quickly emptied, Emma slipped away to the O'Neill's cottage.

Chapter 11

Brendan is Suspended

"THE POLICE?" Deelie cried. "Isn't it bad enough already?"

Emma had found her sitting, Orla in her arms, staring at Brendan as he paced the kitchen, extolling the sins of the English and their unreasonable dislike of the Irish, her news just adding to their distress. Orla picked up on the upset and began crying and hiccupping as Deelie rocked her. Liam, his bottom lip quivering, looked as if he were about to join his sister.

"It's for the best," Emma strove to reassure them as she rubbed Liam's back. "They will soon discover that Brendan couldn't have shot an arrow into the mill and the matter will be settled. I mean really, the whole idea is ridiculous."

"The Irish are always the first to be blamed," Brendan said, his eyes hot at the injustice of it. "It has naught to do with right or wrong. It's always been that way. That policeman is English, isn't he? How do you think that will work out?" It was a rhetorical question.

"I won't be going over there to lunch," Deelie announced suddenly, looking defiant. "I'll not be sitting there, eating their food with them thinking you killed one of them. And I won't be giving them the pleasure of turning us away."

Emma thought showing up and acting as if nothing was wrong might make more sense. Hiding away could be seen as guilt. But she held her counsel when Brendan stared at Deelie as if searching for a suitable response. It turned out he thought much the same as she did.

"We've no reason to be hiding," he said. "I've done nothing to hide for."

"But they'll be thinking it, watching. How can you eat with them?"

"It's only Frank thinking it."

"No, Bren. They'll all be wondering now. They were all there when Mr. Frank called you a murderer. Those women will look at me all pitying or accusing like if I go over there."

"They'll think you don't believe me if you don't go."

Deelie shook her head, bending over Orla. Brendan looked at a loss.

"You could tell them Liam isn't feeling well," Emma suggested to him. "And I'm helping Deelie care for him and Orla. If you want to go."

"It's not like they'd believe it," Brendan said dismissing the idea. "You've got to trust me, Dee," Brendan implored his wife.

"I do trust you. It's them I don't."

"Nor I. But I'm not for letting them beat me down." Deelie shook her head. "Right then. I should get back to work before they send someone to fetch me. You'll stay with her, Emma?"

"I will."

Brendan nodded. He bent and kissed the top of Deelie's head, before taking up his hat. There was a knock on the cottage door. Deelie leapt to her feet, clutching Orla to her, defiance in her eyes and the set of her mouth.

Emma stepped beside her and put an arm around her friend's shoulder. Brendan glanced back at them and opened the door. Rory Felling stepped into the cottage.

Deelie almost sagged with relief at the sight of their friend but the troubled expression on Rory's face did not bode well to Emma. Brendan saw it too.

"What's going on, then?" he asked.

"Declan asked me to bring you a message. He wants you to stay here at the cottage until this matter is sorted."

"I've been condemned already."

Rory shook his head. "No laddie. It's just a precaution. You can't work alongside them right now. You being in their sight would only cause trouble. It'll be over in a few days, you'll see, once the police figure it was an accident." He clapped Brendan on the shoulder. "I'll be seeing you soon."

Brendan closed the door behind Rory and stood with his hand on it, staring at the floor.

Emma was incensed. "Why didn't Declan come and tell you himself? Why send Rory? It's like he's too embarrassed to face you, because he knows you can't have done it and he's just humouring his brother."

"You think that?" Brendan said looking up.

"Yes, and we'll prove it," Emma told him firmly. "You're not the only one Frank suspects. He's already accused several of his brothers of wanting Andrew out of the way because he wasn't supporting what they wanted."

"He'll not tell the police that, so. They'll stick together, you'll see."

"But I can tell the police."

If she could come up with enough suspects it would at least take the focus off Brendan. And who knows, she might be able to prove someone else fired that arrow She already thought Evan and Ruth might have a motive of their own. But really, the whole idea was bizarre. Fire arrows?

"If anyone can do it Emma, you can," Deelie said. She became all businesslike. "But we're going to have to get lunch first. Lamb chops and colcannon, I'm thinking."

The children were soon settled, Orla in her basket and Liam with some toys on the bedroom floor. Deelie put water on to boil for the vegetables and Emma set to peeling potatoes at the table.

"What is all this about shooting with bows and arrows, anyway?" Emma asked Brendan. "It sounded as if finding an arrowhead wasn't anything unusual here. I shouldn't be surprised, really, I suppose. Archery is something people with leisure and money can afford to indulge in. I've just never known anyone who has."

"It's not unusual here," Brendan said.

"What do they shoot?"

"Birds. Targets sometimes."

"But a fire arrow? Sounds like something from medieval times when marauders laid siege to a castle."

Brendan, who was leaning against the doorway to the bedroom, shook his head.

"It would take some skill, surely, to put an arrow through one of those openings. They aren't all that big. And with the sails passing over." She pictured what she'd seen when she was in the mill and Jack Brighten turned the sail to make the repair. In the bedroom, Liam was banging a spoon on a pan.

"The sails are only on one side and there are windows all round," Deelie said, ever practical.

"Of course, there are. So which side were the sails on when it happened?" Emma tried to remember what Andrew had told her about moving the cap and the sails to get best advantage of the wind.

"The wind was from the south," Brendan said.

"Right, and the explosion blew the sails forward toward the trees in the garden. That meant the window openings at the back of the mill would have been clear."

"So, if someone hid down in the – what you call it – where the river used to go."

"Billabong."

"Down there, no one would see them," Deelie said.

"Perhaps," she said. It would have to be checked. "How far can you shoot an arrow? Is that bank too far?" She shook her head, frustrated. "We don't know enough. Who could I ask?" The brothers would know of course, but they weren't likely to appreciate her asking questions. "Oh, for goodness sake," she said, as a thought occurred to her. She turned from the fire where she was stirring the vegetables. "We're being very stupid. I don't know how Frank can even think it was you, Brendan. You've got to be able to use a bow to have done it."

He was an Irish farm labourer. When would he have learned to shoot a bow and arrow? It was a sport for the upper classes with time on their hands. She had shot down Frank's suspicions already.

"Give me that, now," Brendan said, taking the spoon from Liam.

He picked the boy up and threw him over his shoulder, making him giggle. Emma was relieved the banging had stopped. She marvelled at the way parents could tune out noise like that. Deelie turned the lamb chops sizzling in the pan. It took a moment for her to realise that neither were saying anything. In fact, Brendan hadn't been saying more than a few words in answer to her questions, leaving the discussion to Deelie. She'd thought it was because he didn't know anything about archery.

"Don't tell me you know how to use a bow and arrow," she said quietly, berating herself for being guilty of snobbery, and feeling a little sick.

Brendan set Liam on his feet. "Ian taught me," he said resignation in his voice.

Emma sighed. "I see. I just assumed..."

"It was a fair thought, Emma. It would never have crossed my mind I might do that, before coming here."

"So, you can tell me then, if someone could have shot an arrow into the mill from below the billabong?"

"They could."

"How much skill would it take?"

"Those windows are not as small a target as a bird."

"And you can hit a bird?"

"Often enough. If it's not moving."

Emma let out a heartfelt sigh. Little wonder they were so concerned. They needed other motives and other suspects.

"What can you tell me about the brothers, Brendan? Did Declan want to take over the place from Andrew so badly that he would kill him?"

Deelie shuddered. "It's not natural, brothers behaving that way."

"Even the Bible has the story of Cain and Abel," Emma reminded her. "It's the closest of relationships that generate the most passion." She had seen enough of that in her life already.

"They do talk a lot about what they should be doing," Brendan said. "They all have their own ideas. Andrew was set on wheat and flour. Wool brings in good money but they're carrying as many sheep as the land can take. Andrew's favourite words on that was acres per sheep, not sheep per acre."

"Did anyone want to increase the flocks?"

Brendan shrugged. "Not really. Mostly it was Evan arguing for money to set up his vineyard. He talked about an orchard as well. Soft fruits for the Adelaide market."

No wonder Andrew was interested in a riverboat. "And Andrew wouldn't provide the money?"

"You heard Rory. It couldn't be done all at once. But I don't know. Andrew said once he didn't think there was enough water in the river in the summer." He shrugged. "Perhaps he might never have agreed."

"And Andrew was spending money on the new mill. Evan wasn't happy about that, was he?" Emma said, reading between the lines of the conversation she had heard in the barn on her first day.

"No, but…" Brendan hesitated. "They didn't hate one another, Emma. I've sat at lunch and listened to them for some time now and worked beside them, too. I can't see it."

"It will be about that man," Deelie said. Emma noticed her friend never graced Jack Brighten with a name. He was always 'that man.'

Brendan's lips thinned, and he thumped the wall with his fist. "No one would have blown up the mill to get at him. He wasn't worth it. Andy would've sent him on his way if it were bad enough."

"Or sent us, Bren." Deelie dissolved into tears. Brendan looked at his wife helplessly.

"Come on," Emma encouraged. "We'll feel better when we've eaten."

After lunch, Emma helped Deelie clean up in the kitchen. Liam went down for his afternoon nap but instead of resting, Deelie pulled out the scales and started measuring flour and sugar and beating eggs.

Emma offered to help but was answered with a shake of the head. Deelie clearly wasn't in the mood for company. Brendan took himself out the back and was soon heard chopping firewood. Everyone had their own way of dealing with adversity. They weren't going to go hungry or cold anyway.

Chapter 12

Emma Lines Up Her Suspects

EMMA FOUND HER latest notebook in the bottom of her bag and took herself out to the bench in the garden. She could have sat out front of the cottages but in the homestead garden there was always the possibility of someone coming by she could speak to.

She couldn't imagine the brothers talking to her about what had happened. They wouldn't turn on one another in front of Lieutenant Forrester either, but he might tell her what they had to say if she had information she could share. She could speak with the women and see what that turned up. Mrs. Fowler, the maids, Ann Russell the schoolteacher, Ruth and Naomi. The latter two were Lockwoods, certainly, but only by marriage. They might talk to her.

She opened her notebook and began to make a list. Regardless of Brendan's opinion, she couldn't rule out anyone.

Victims:

Andrew Lockwood - holding the purse strings and

making decisions that affected everyone.

Jack Brighten - Conflict with Brendan. Anyone else? Generally unliked, according to Rory.

<u>*Suspects*</u>*:*

Mrs. Lockwood - extremely unlikely.

Barbara - Did she have a grudge against her older brother? wanted more say in what happened about the place?

Declan - did he want to be head of the family and in control of the property?

Evan - needed money to develop his vineyard. Andrew wouldn't give it to him.

Frank - What did he want? Why was he so sure Andrew wouldn't be so careless?

Harold - the aggressive one. What did he want?

Ian - just because he'd been injured didn't mean he didn't do it. Setting up his easel right there would have been a good cover. Motive? Was he expected to give up painting and become a proper farmer?

All the Lockwoods had opportunity as far as she knew. And they could have had an issue with Jack Brighten, but she doubted they would have blown up the mill to get at him and risk killing one of their own. No. If one of the family had done this, it would have been Andrew who was the target.

That brought her to Evan and his aborted visit to Ruth's cottage yesterday. He might deny wanting

Andrew out of the way so he could develop his vineyard, but what about wanting him out of the way to
get to his wife? And if so, why now?

She was going to have to tell Lieutenant Forrester
about her suspicions. Get him investigating Evan and
leave Brendan alone. She could help check on alibis,
see who might be lying about where they were. She
continued with her suspect list.

Brendan O'Neill - opportunity. Motive - hated Jack
Brighten.

Rory Felling - opportunity. Problem with Jack
Brighten? More likely to confront him than blow
up the mill.

Bricklayers - opportunity. Motive? Leave for the
Lieutenant.

Deelie O'Neill - alibi. Emma was with her all
morning.

Janet Felling - opportunity. Had Jack Brighten
bothered her? Or Andrew? Rory would have
dealt with it but can't see it.

Mrs. Fowler and the maids - probably no
opportunity given their work schedule, but they
would have to be checked out. It wouldn't be the
first time a master had taken advantage of a
female servant.

Ann Russell - busy with the school children?
Motive - Ditto above.

Ruth Lockwood - she had been with her and Deelie.

Had Evan done it on her behalf? Problems with Jack Brighten?

Naomi Lockwood – seen coming from her cottage at the time of the explosion. Motive - Jealousy, an affair, spurned? Ditto re Jack Brighten.

Apart from herself, Deelie, and Mrs. Lockwood, she couldn't rule anyone out completely. If the two Lockwood wives were involved, someone else had done it for them. She remembered seeing one of the maids coming from a cottage at the time, too. The one whose name she didn't know. She made a note on her list.

"You're looking very industrious." Emma looked up to see Ann Russell standing before her, hands on hips. She was dressed in her schoolmistress costume, the black contrasting heavily with her pale complexion. Emma instinctively closed her notebook. "We've not managed to be properly introduced given what's happened lately, but I'm sure we both know who the other one is. We missed you at lunch today."

Looking up at Ann's sharp features she found herself staring at the nostrils of her up-tilted nose, a disconcerting view.

"Won't you sit down?" Emma said, wondering at the attitude and choosing to ignore the reference to lunch.

"How is everyone treating you?" Ann asked as she sat. "Very well, I imagine, given who you are."

Emma looked at her with some surprise. "Who I am is a guest, so why wouldn't I be treated with courtesy?"

"Oh, not just any guest. But nothing will come of that for the moment after what has happened."

"I have no idea what you are talking about, Miss Russell

"I see. Well, no need to worry. The seed has been sown, anyway. Tell me, have you met all the brothers?"

"I've seen them, but I've only spoken to Andrew and Frank."

"You spoke to Frank?"

"Briefly. He was searching the ruins the day after the fire, terribly upset. He's found the evidence he was searching for now. What do you think of it?"

Ann looked down at her hands clenched in her lap. "He is upset. He thought the sun rose and set on Andrew. He will get over it in due course. But," she said looking up, "Ruth is the one who is grieving the most. I can't imagine how it must feel to lose a husband."

Emma wasn't about to discuss grieving for a husband with Ann. "I find the whole idea of archery interesting," she said instead. "It seems to have been a popular occupation with the Lockwoods."

"Oh, goodness yes. They've been shooting arrows all over the place since they were children. Even the women. I mean, the men like to teach the women how to hold the bow and chock the arrow. A good excuse to put their arms around them." She giggled.

"My goodness. That's worse than croquet," Emma said lightly. "Men and women off flirting in the shrubbery when they are supposed to be looking for a lost ball. Well, I just hope they can discover what really happened. I don't imagine it will be easy."

"Oh, I'm sure it will come out as an accident," Ann said. "That arrowhead was no doubt lying about since forever. I understand the good Lieutenant is coming tomorrow morning to sort it out. He may even want to speak with you again." She looked slyly at Emma.

"Possibly," Emma replied, ignoring the insinuation. "How long have you been teaching here?"

"This is my second year."

"Is it a good position?"

"It's better than many in the country, I must say."

"So, you intend staying a while?"

Ann smiled rather smugly. "Oh, I think so. Unless you ever need a teacher at your place. That might be interesting, too."

"I doubt we will. But what do you do in your spare time when you aren't teaching?"

"I read a lot," she said. "I have an Aunt in Nottingham who sends me packages of books several times a year. I just love the Bronte sisters and Jane Austen. So romantic. But Anthony Trollope is my favourite author right now."

"And mine." Emma wondered if Ann might liken Trollope's landed gentry to the Lockwoods and yearn to be a part of that lifestyle. "I imagine you must spend some time with the parents of your pupils, too," she said, hoping for some information on Andrew and Declan and their wives.

Ann gave her another sly, sideways glance. "Oh, I see," she said. "You want inside information to assist your plans, don't you?" She wagged her finger at Emma as if she were scolding a pupil. "Oh no. You will have to do that on your own. You already have enough going for you." She stood. "I have lessons to prepare."

Before Emma could recover, she had walked off. What an odd young woman. Emma wasn't sure what to make of her, except she didn't think she would trust her with a secret. Ann was sure to make oblique comments about anything she knew. She had hoped Ian might come out onto the verandah again and she could talk to him, but it wasn't to be, so she went back to the cottage.

Brendan was sitting at the table with *The Swiss Family Robinson* in his hands, though whether he was actually reading or just staring at the same page, Emma wasn't sure. The cottage smelt of fresh baked bread and something with cinnamon that turned out to be apple pie. The only ones talking, though, were the children and they weren't saying anything of much help.

Emma hadn't been long in when Mrs. Fowler arrived with a casserole. She didn't come inside but just handed it in at the door.

"You may as well have this, as you didn't come over for lunch today."

Deelie took the dish. "Thank you, Mrs. Fowler. That's awfully kind of you."

"It's chicken. It wouldn't have kept past tomorrow, anyway. Even the condemned man has to eat."

Deelie looked as if the air had been knocked out of her.

"She certainly has a way with words, that woman," Emma commented.

Chapter 13

A Matter of Gates

HAVING HEARD from Ann that the good Lieutenant was due that morning, Emma's first objective was to speak to him before he started his investigation. Immediately after breakfast she left Deelie with a pile of laundry to deal with. Brendan was getting the fire going under the copper, and with him confined to the cottage she felt Deelie had enough help with the children.

The strained atmosphere in the cottage wasn't conducive to a social visit anyway. Not that she blamed them. The sooner the matter was resolved the better for everyone concerned. That was something she was better equipped to be helping with than the family wash.

Over by the new mill, the bricklayers were setting up for the day's work, carting bricks up the scaffolding and mixing mortar. They had almost reached the top. It would soon be time to set up the workings inside. She saw Frank ahead of her entering the barn and slowed her step so as not to draw his attention, and then quickened her pace as she passed between the barn and the homestead, reaching the track on the other side.

In the paddock on the far side, Frank was putting a draught horse into the shafts of the flat bed wagon. It appeared more work was to be done on clearing the mill today. Past the horse paddock, Emma could see the pile of mill debris stacked for burning.

She set off up the track, past the homestead and the schoolhouse, and the ordered backyard of the cottages. The Mallee landscape of red sand peppered with multi-stemmed eucalypts and hummock-shaped porcupine grass effectively deterred wandering off the track. There were no landmarks to guide you back.

A large frill-necked lizard, sunning himself in the open, startled her. Equally startled by her approach, it raised itself on its hind legs and raced away into the bush, frill flaring. A lone kookaburra burst out into mocking laughter as she passed.

"I'm glad someone is enjoying themselves," Emma muttered brushing flies from her face. She broke a leafy switch from a Mallee shrub and waved it about. She was still keeping the flies at bay when, about ten minutes later, she heard the jingle of harness and thudding of hooves on sand.

"You are going somewhere?" Lieutenant Forrester asked, eyebrows raised as he stopped beside her, knowing it was miles to the nearest habitation.

Emma tried to ignore how well he looked in the saddle, his military background obvious. Behind him, two black troopers stopped a little way off.

"I was hoping to have a word with you before you speak to the family," Emma said. "I feel there are some things you should know that the family may not tell you."

He considered her for a moment. "Very well." He sent the troopers on ahead and dismounted, bringing the reins down over his horse's head.

"I don't know if you are expecting to find any evidence at the site," Emma told him as they walked on. "I imagine that's why you brought the troopers, but the area's been washed clean by the rain and much trampled, and they've started on clearing up."

"I didn't expect any less, although I did see the damage when I was here on Saturday, but the troopers will be making a wider search." She would be surprised if they found anything. There had been time for the killer, if there was one, to remove any evidence. "What are you so keen I should know?"

"Well, yesterday, when the arrowhead was found, Frank Lockwood turned on his brothers and accused them of wanting Andrew Lockwood dead for various reasons."

"I see. And what reasons may they be?"

Where was the friendly man she had spoken to at the wake? His professional demeanour was in full force today.

"Declan may have wanted to take over control of River Bend and Evan wants funds to develop his vineyard which Andrew was slow in providing."

"And you are telling me this in order to take the focus off your friend O'Neill."

"Well, the brothers aren't likely to tell you these things themselves, are they? They'll close ranks and look for a scapegoat. Someone outside the family. What I'm saying is, there's more to it."

"There usually is. And then, of course, it could have been an accident and the arrowhead have nothing to do with it."

"You still have to prove it," Emma pointed out. "You still have to clear Brendan. And everyone else."

"Are you telling me how to do my job, now, Mrs. Berry?"

"Of course not. It's just..."

"It's just that you are trying to protect your friend. I understand. I do know what I am doing."

Emma wasn't so sure of that. How many murders had he investigated? He hadn't done so well in Hilda Zeller's case. Well, if he didn't want her help, he could find out for himself that Brendan could use a bow. But it meant she also couldn't mention being useful with a bow and arrow was the most obvious thing to find out about everyone.

"I'm not trying to protect Brendan, as you put it, just make sure you are aware of what else is going on. It has also come to my attention that Evan Lockwood may have some romantic interest in Andrew's wife, Ruth."

"Well, passion is as likely a motive as any, providing we find we need one. What evidence do you have for thinking that?"

"I saw him leaving her cottage by the back door on the evening of the explosion. And he was heading toward her cottage on Sunday but saw me and changed direction."

"Did he now?" Emma detected a note of amusement in his voice and gave an exaggerated sigh. He cleared his throat. "I will look into it," he said.

She could see the back of the schoolhouse through the trees, now. She stopped walking, forcing the Lieutenant to do the same.

"And another thing." She hesitated, unsure how he would take it but decided there was nothing to lose. "I'm going to speak to the women. Ruth and Naomi Lockwood couldn't have been involved themselves as I know where they were at the time of the explosion, but that's not to say someone wasn't acting for them. If anything, they may be able to provide more information on relationships that could provide motives. And I can check alibis. The women are more likely to speak to me, and the men to you, after all. I'm hoping we can share what we find."

Lieutenant Forrester ran his hand down the side of his horse's head. He seemed to be warring with himself. Go it alone or accept her offer, which she was certain he could see made sense.

"We can try that," he said eventually. "I will be speaking to everyone, men and women alike, but you may pick up on something I don't hear about. I trust you won't hold anything back in the hope of protecting O'Neill."

"Of course not." Emma hoped her face wouldn't betray her because it was exactly what she was doing. She hoped it wouldn't come back to bite her.

The Lieutenant nodded and mounted his horse, then looked down at her, his hazel eyes serious. Emma felt herself suddenly a little short of breath under his gaze.

"Just promise me you'll be careful. Please."

Emma nodded. As he trotted off, she had a fleeting image of life as a policeman's wife, assisting with her husband's investigations. "Ridiculous," she muttered, shaking her head to dispel the thought.

Emma waited until Lieutenant Forrester had disappeared between the barn and the homestead before she went on. As she got closer to the buildings, she saw there was a gate she hadn't noticed before in the fence near the schoolhouse. That would save her going around the homestead and through the side garden. Before she opened it, she looked over to see if Alfie were anywhere nearby but couldn't see him.

The gate opened with a squeak. Closing it behind her she made her way across the grass heading for Deelie's cottage.

"Did you enjoy your walk?"

Ann Russell's voice came unexpectedly from beneath the peppermint willow, startling her. She peered into the shadows. Ann was sitting at a table, a cup of tea and an empty plate in front of her, a book in her hand, a shawl warming her shoulders. Emma thought sitting in the sun would have been more comfortable.

"I did, thank you."

"I would have thought the river was a more pleasant place to walk than that dusty track. But then you never know who you might meet, coming and going, do you? Quite a handsome man, that Lieutenant."

"There are a lot of handsome men in the world," Emma replied walking on.

Ann's laugh followed her. So much for speaking to the Lieutenant in private. No doubt it would be all over the place by lunch time that she had waylaid him on the track. It wasn't surprising Ann sat in the shadows. Better to observe unnoticed.

As Emma passed Naomi and Declan's cottage their two older children Jonathan and Laura, came out and dawdled off in the direction of the schoolhouse. Jonathan whistled, and Alfie came dashing from somewhere out back, cavorting around and slowing their progress, which was probably what the boy intended.

Emma heard a knock, and looking back, saw Laura at her Aunt Ruth's cottage. If she was inquiring about her cousins coming to school today she was to be disappointed, as she was turned away by the maid whose name Emma still didn't know.

The gate by the schoolhouse had Emma thinking. Someone could go out that way and down to the river then cut back along to below the mill, hidden by the trees. Perhaps there was a gate in the fence on the other side past Deelie and Brendan's cottage. That was an even closer route to the river, though you would have to cross the yard, front or back, to get there and run the risk of being seen from the cottages. Unless you were Brendan.

Emma walked down the far side of Deelie's cottage in the gap between it and the side fence. Deelie was busy in the washhouse from which clouds of steam were issuing. There was no sign of Brendan or Liam outside.

Without disturbing her friend, she started to poke about behind the greenery. It didn't take long to find the gate near the back corner of the cottage half hidden by shrubbery. It opened without a squeak. She put a finger on top of the hinge and found a little oil. Someone wanted to come and go quietly here. It would be another mark against Brendan if the

Lieutenant thought to check access to the river from this side.

"Emma?" She started guiltily at the sound of Brendan's voice behind her. "What are you doing?"

"Oh, I, um..."

He had a strange expression on his face. Somewhere between sadness and anger. She wasn't sure which emotion was uppermost. What did she know about him really? Violence could lurk beneath that pleasant exterior just waiting to be unleashed. She knew he had a grudge against Jack Brighten. He could just as easily have disliked Andrew Lockwood and all he stood for, as one of those English landholders he blamed for Irish woes. Did he see her family as one?

"I saw there was a gate at the other end of the yard near the schoolhouse and just wondered if there was one here as well. I hadn't noticed it before. It's very convenient. Do you go down to the river often?" She was babbling.

"Do you think I snuck down there and shot an arrow into the mill?"

Emma gulped. "I don't know, Brendan," she had to admit. "I think a man, or a woman, is capable of almost anything if the thing they treasure most is threatened."

Brendan's face darkened. "How am I to convince the police when even my friends don't believe me?"

Emma didn't know how to respond. She wanted desperately to believe for Deelie's sake.

"Where were you when the mill exploded?" That could clear him immediately, especially if he had a witness to his whereabouts.

Brendan flushed and looked away. "I go by the gate to check my fish trap."

"You were doing that at the time?" Why not just say so.

"No. Not at that time." Emma waited for more, but it wasn't forthcoming.

"Lieutenant Forrester will be asking you the same question. He will expect an answer."

"I will tell him."

Something he could tell the Lieutenant that he couldn't tell her. Was he somewhere he shouldn't have been? With someone he shouldn't have been with? Was there more behind Jack Brighten's taunting?

"What are you two talking about?"

Emma turned quickly. Deelie, her face flushed from the heat in the wash house and her hands full with a basket of wet washing, was looking at them quizzically. Emma attempted a smile, but Brendan spoke first.

"Fish. I was thinking to check the trap for fish for lunch." Was that the quick tongue of a man who lied easily?

"That would be nice Bren. You can fry them up while I finish the wash." She looked around frowning. "Where's Liam?"

"What? Oh, he was just here a moment ago."

"Honestly, Bren..."

"I'll look out front," Emma said glad to escape them both. She saw the boy almost immediately as she rounded the front of the cottage. He was rattling the gate leading to the garden. Alfie was standing on his back legs beside him, helping.

"He's out here," she called. "You both trying to get out, are you," she said when she reached them. "You've got a lovely big yard to run about in already, you know that?"

"Da, da," Liam cried out.

"Da's here," Brendan said coming up behind them. "Confined to quarters just the same."

He picked Liam up and sat him on his shoulder. The little boy crowed. Emma turned away, thinking she should go help Deelie with the wash as she was unsure what else she could say to Brendan.

"I thought of it, Emma," Brendan said. "I thought of it, I can say." Emma turned back to him as he stared out at nothing. "I'd lie awake at night thinking of ways to shut him up, him and his words. Lure him to the river and drown him, beat his head in. It seemed to be all I could think about."

He set Liam on his feet and looked straight at her.

"But then I realised I could lose everything – Deelie, the children, my own life. I decided I couldn't let some blighted scoundrel push me to that. So, I thought the only thing we could do was leave here, when Orla was a little older and I had learned to read and write well enough to get some other kind of work, in a town somewhere. Someplace where you aren't living so close in with other people. I just kept out of his way as much as I could, and kept hoping something would change, Andrew might get rid of him. Something." He sighed heavily.

"Well, something did happen, now, didn't it? It frightened me. I admit it did. It was almost as if I'd done it myself, brought it on him by wishing, I'd thought on it so long. I felt as if I caused it, that I murdered the man like Frank is saying. Can you understand that?"

Emma could understand it. Anthony Trollope had even written of one of his characters feeling guilty of the theft of the Eustace diamonds because he was one of those suspected of being involved, despite his innocence. Brendan's story had a ring of truth to it.

"Fortunately, you can't be hanged for wishing," she said.

"But how do I prove I didn't shoot that arrow into the mill?"

"I don't know why you can't tell me where you were at the time if it will clear you, but if you can tell the Lieutenant that will do. Was anyone with you?"

"No, of course not."

Emma didn't know why 'of course not.' She just hoped the alibi was strong enough if he had no one to confirm it.

Chapter 14

Checking Alibis

AS EMMA HUNG out a long line of diapers, she wondered how the Lieutenant was getting on with his questioning of the Lockwood brothers. All she had to show so far was more evidence against Brendan, circumstantial though it may be. She desperately needed to find something that pointed in another direction.

Alfie raced up distracting her thoughts. He leapt at the washing, just missing a pair of trousers. Emma grabbed the prop and tried to set the line a little higher as she scolded him. He took no notice and leapt again. Emma was afraid if the wind caught the washing, the prop could tilt and bring the clothes within reach.

"Is anyone responsible for training Alfie?" she asked Deelie when she returned to the washhouse.

"Not that I know."

"It's no wonder he's such a scamp. Who feeds him?"

"Mrs. Fowler looks after that. He does well from the kitchen scraps. He has a bed on the front verandah of the schoolhouse. Ann tried having him inside, but he chewed the buttons off her best boots."

"How annoying."

"It turned out fine. Ruth gave her an almost full packet of silver buttons to replace them. Now Ann has silver buttons on both pair of boots, her everyday pair, and her Sunday best. She's well pleased with herself." Deelie glanced at Emma as she said this and they both laughed. Boot buttons. It was the smallest things that gave the most pleasure.

"Well, someone should be training Alfie. If he learns to knock down the clothesline props, you'll have a real mess on your hands."

"Oh, he's already grabbed a diaper out of my wash basket," Deelie said. "Right quick he is. Perhaps Bren could take him in hand. Give him something to do," she added her voice trailing off.

"It'll work out," Emma consoled trying to sound more confident than she felt. It niggled that Brendan wouldn't tell her where he had been when the mill exploded.

After lunch, when Deelie was busy with the children, she asked Brendan what he knew about fire arrows.

"I don't know anything," he insisted. "No one ever spoke of them to me. Ian would know."

"Would he talk to me, do you think?" He might have remembered something useful by now and she wanted to assess whether he could have been involved somehow.

Brendan shrugged. "He would talk to me if I could get to see him."

"Which is a bit difficult right now, isn't it? I'm not sure how welcome I would be at the homestead, either. Mrs. Lockwood wasn't happy with what I had to say to her about Frank and his accusations. Now he's found what he thinks is proof, well, I'm not sure what she might be thinking."

"She must be very worried," Deelie said from the bedroom.

"I'm sure she's that. I told the Lieutenant what Frank had to say. I can't see the family giving the Lieutenant any information that might implicate one of their own. I told him I will be speaking to everyone I can, and we will share what we find." At least she hoped they would be. He hadn't exactly been forthcoming on that part. "Can you tell me where everyone was working that morning, Brendan?" she asked.

"Frank and I were in the stable, oiling the horse leathers." He had no trouble telling her that so he must have been somewhere else at the time of the explosion.

"The stable? That's the building at the back of the horse paddock on the other side of the track?"

"That's it."

"And anyone else?"

"Evan had gone to potter around in his vineyard. It's almost time to start the pruning. I don't know where Declan was."

"What about Harold." Brendan shook his head. "Did you see Ian?"

"No, but he'd told me he was going to draw the mill at some time while it was still standing, so I suppose that was what he was doing when he got hurt."

"You said he did that portrait of Mr. Lockwood in the dining room, Deelie. Is it a good likeness, do you know?"

"Janet says so."

"Ian painted it from memory," Brendan said. "After his father had died."

If it was true to life, Emma thought the portrait might say a great deal about Ian's relationship with his father. If what she'd seen in the painting was what Ian remembered, his father hadn't been showering favour on his youngest son's art. Did Ian have a similar relationship with Andrew? She couldn't discount him. She hoped Ian's friendship with Brendan, teaching him archery, hadn't been to make Brendan a convenient scapegoat for his own actions.

<><><>

EMMA CROSSED the yard to the garden gate. There must be someone she could talk to about fire arrows, even if she had to sit in the garden all afternoon until someone came by, Barbara, or Ann perhaps. Alfie escorted her.

"You have to stay, Alfie," Emma told him her hand on the gate. He sat and looked at her, head cocked to one side, eyes bright. "Yes, you know perfectly well what I mean. You're a bright little dog, aren't you?" She bent and scratched his head. "You just need to be taught to behave."

She lifted the latch. Alfie stood up eagerly, tail wagging at the sound. "No." Emma, bending forward, put one hand out as she opened the gate with the other. "Stay." She quickly backed through the opening and shut the gate before he had a chance to slip by. "Good boy. You deserve a treat."

She would ask Mrs. Fowler if she had something. That would give her an excuse to visit. As she turned, she all but bumped into a young man standing on the path behind her.

"Oh, Mr. Lockwood. I do apologise."

Ian Lockwood looked down at her, the side of his face still bandaged and taped. Tall and slim like his brothers, but with clear blue eyes, long blonde hair, and a scarf casually thrown around his neck. It probably took him ages to get the casual look of the artist exactly right. Emma didn't think he could be more than nineteen which made the slightly superior look on his face annoying.

"Mrs. Berry, I presume. You aren't trying to teach that beast some manners, are you? That's a thankless task. Others have tried, you know."

"Well, I don't know what anyone has tried, but I think he'd be quite biddable with the right touch."

"Yours, you mean."

"Oh no. I'm only here for a few days. I'm glad to see you up and about," she said leaving a subject that wasn't about to go anywhere.

He gave a small bow. "Almost as good as ever. I will even have a scar to show for it."

Emma acknowledged his ironic tone with a small smile and became serious again.

"Everyone was quite concerned about you. I'm sorry about the loss of your brother."

"Yes, not having someone complain and grumble at me all the time is a great loss." She wasn't sure if he was putting on a front, feigning a blasé attitude, or it was just lack of self-confidence due to his youth.

"Was it really so bad?" Emma asked remembering he was still high on her list of suspects.

Ian gave a theatrical sigh. "Well, it wasn't good. Andy couldn't understand anyone wanted to live differently. I didn't contribute anything. That was his main complaint. Just like Father." Emma pictured a little boy wanting approval and not getting any from the male authorities in his life. "It would have been better if Frank hadn't found that arrowhead."

"You think someone really did shoot a fire arrow into the mill and cause the explosion?"

Ian shrugged. "It isn't likely to be proved one way or the other, is it? Unless someone confesses."

"But if Brendan didn't do it that needs to be proved, too, doesn't it? You can't have suspicion hanging over people forever."

Ian stared at her for a moment. "No one really believes it was done on purpose," he said, with clear emphasis on the 'really.'

"Your brother Frank does."

Ian shrugged. "Frank is the only one." Emma wasn't so sure. Ian cleared his throat. "Do you think I could see Bren? He's not mad, is he? It's not my fault Dec's made him stay home."

"I'm sure he would like to see you. I'd like to speak with you myself."

"Oh? If you want to find out what happened, you're wasting your time. I didn't see anything. I've already told the Lieutenant. I was just sitting there one minute and knocked down the next."

"Well, come and talk to Brendan, anyway," she said, opening the gate carefully and grabbing Alfie's collar as he tried to slip by.

"Good boy." She gave Alfie a quick pat as Ian followed her through and shut the gate behind him. "I wanted to ask you about fire arrows," she said.

"They're properly called flaming arrows, not fire arrows," Ian corrected her, "and I've already told that Lieutenant all I know."

"Do you have any objection to telling me?"

"I suppose not."

Naomi came out of her cottage just then with Norman in her arms. She looked a little surprised to see them but just nodded as she headed toward the back door of the homestead.

"Bother."

"Is something wrong?"

"She'll tell Dec I was here, and he'll be on at me."

"Because you were talking to me? You were told you couldn't talk to me? Or Brendan?"

"Well... no. No one actually said it."

"That's all right then," Emma said briskly walking on. She wasn't about to humour Ian's put on airs, but she did want to talk to him. When Emma entered the cottage, she found Brendan sitting at the table at work on his letters again.

"You have a visitor," she announced.

"Ian." The look Brendan gave him was tinged with trepidation. Ian put his hand out and Brendan stood and shook it warmly, his face relaxing into a smile. "It's grand to see you. Do I need to tell you I had nothing to do with what's happened?"

"I never thought you had. It's Dec's idea to shut you up. No one ever asks me what I think."

Brendan shrugged. "So, what have the police been up to? I haven't seen anyone."

"Asking lots of questions and turning the place upside down. It's hell," Ian said, dropping into a chair. "The fellow wants to know where everyone was down to the last second before the mill blew itself to pieces with everyone in it."

Brendan looked a little shocked at Ian's words. Before he could respond, there was a small cry from the sleepout and Deelie popped her head around the door.

"Could you take yourselves outside or talk more quietly," she said, making it more of a statement than a question. "I'm trying to get Liam to sleep." The cottage was so small ordinary voices could be heard all over.

"Sure, sure," Brendan soothed. "Come on. We'd best sit out for now."

"You won't mind if I join you," Emma said not leaving room for a refusal. "I told Ian I wanted to know about these flaming arrows."

Brendan carried a chair out for Emma, and he and Ian sat on the bench.

"So, tell me first what I want to know," Emma said. "Then I can leave you two to talk together." Time was running out. It was Tuesday already and Tom Gulbis was to come and collect her after lunch Thursday.

"Like I told the Lieutenant, flaming arrows were used in medieval times to set fire to towns or castles under siege."

"And they worked?" Brendan asked in surprise. "How did the flame stay alight during the flight?"

"Ah," Ian raised a finger. "Clever question. The Lieutenant didn't ask me that. Clearly, he has never fired an arrow in anger."

"So, why doesn't it get blown out?" Emma asked.

"Because you use a lighter bow that doesn't shoot the arrow as fast. Less wind resistance."

"But who here would know that?" Emma asked. "Are you in the habit of shooting flaming arrows at River Bend?"

"Well, not after the last time. Ma has banned them." Ian looked down at his feet, seeming reluctant to say more.

"Please. We need to know anything that might be relevant," Emma said. "We won't repeat it if it isn't."

"It's embarrassing." He sighed. "We had a display for Ma's birthday. Last August. A clear cold night, no wind, perfect. We set ourselves up down below the horse paddock, three on each side facing away at an angle. We planned to have our arrows cross over in midflight. Looks quite spectacular. But one arrow went astray. It landed in the hay shed and burnt it completely."

"Oh, my goodness. Whose arrow went astray? It wasn't yours, was it?"

Ian nodded. "It had been my idea to do it, too. We hadn't done it since Father died." His brothers obviously listened to him sometimes then, whatever he might claim.

"So, if your mother has banned the use of flaming arrows no one would be out shooting them for fun, would they?" Emma said. "I mean, they are obviously dangerous. How easy would it be to start a bush fire and put your home at risk? And you wouldn't be out hunting birds with a flaming arrow, would you?"

"That would be just stupid," Ian agreed. "We only ever used them at night, and it was only a handful of times, when the conditions were right. There's not much point in the daylight."

"Whose idea was it for you all to be involved with archery?" She didn't think it had been Mrs. Lockwood's.

"Father. He was mad keen on it. He'd been involved with some re-enactment group back in England when he was younger. He taught us all to hunt with bow and arrow before we were allowed guns." He stopped for a moment. "No one would shoot an arrow into the mill really, would they? Dec says the arrowhead must have been lying around and has nothing to do with the fire." He looked from one to the other for reassurance.

"That'll be the right of it," Brendan said stoutly. Whether he believed it Emma didn't know.

"Can you tell me who else was here when you put on that display for your mother? Who would have seen it?" Perhaps there was someone outside River Bend who could be involved.

"Well, the same people who are here now, I suppose."

"Except us," Brendan said. "It was November when we came here. I'd never heard of flaming arrows before this." Ian glanced quickly at Brendan and away again. It seemed Ian thought he had.

"No, but everyone else..." Ian paused to consider. "All the family, Mrs. Fowler, the maids, Ann Russell, we were all here then."

"The men building the new mill wouldn't have been here, would they?"

"No."

"Had anyone else been invited to celebrate your mother's birthday?"

"Oh, yeah. The Wilsons were here, Doc Wilson and his wife and their daughter, Zoe. And Lizzie." He blushed slightly. Ah, young love. No wonder his hand had been shaky on the bow with Lizzie watching. And no wonder he was embarrassed at the result. "And Mr. Gulbis, of course. Luckily for me. Andy had to behave himself in front of them and he'd calmed down a bit by the following afternoon. He was really mad about the hay shed." Emma didn't doubt it.

"One more thing. Who at River Bend knows how to use a bow?"

Ian seemed surprised by the question. "Everyone."

"All your family, you mean?"

"No, everyone."

"What, even the maids and Mrs. Fowler?"

"Yes. Well, Gladys. Holly and Maudie haven't been here as long. We go out on a Sunday afternoon and shoot targets down below the horse paddock, about once a month or so, just to keep our eye in, you know. Father used to organise it and Andy kept it up. It's a lot of fun. We did it a few weeks back. Mrs. Fowler isn't so keen after the hay shed thing, so she hasn't let Holly and Maudie learn. Yet anyway. I could…" He stopped, and a tinge of colour crept over his face.

Was he thinking of teaching the maids to use a bow as Ann had described? Or of teaching Lizzie? But if what Ian said was true, and she had no reason to doubt it, no one could be ruled out. Which meant where everyone was at the time of the explosion had become of utmost importance.

Chapter 15

Ruth's Story

IT WAS NEARING time for afternoon tea when Emma finally knocked on the front door of Ruth Lockwood's cottage. She could hear children playing out in the backyard, lessons over for the day. She wondered if Ruth's older two, Katherine and Margaret she recalled, had been allowed to join their cousins.

It was Ruth herself who answered the door. She wasn't wearing the unflattering black mourning outfit she had worn at the wake and appeared to have just got out of bed. Dressed in a loose, brightly coloured silk wrapper, made fussy with bows and frills, her hair tied back with a pink ribbon, Emma's first impression was of a badly wrapped Christmas present. Her second was that Ruth had been expecting someone else and was disappointed on seeing who her visitor was.

"Hello, Ruth," Emma greeted her. "I hope I'm not intruding. I wanted to call and offer my condolences."

"Please, come in," Ruth said soulfully. "I was just about to have some tea."

The front door opened directly into a bright sitting room. A fire warmed the room. There was a large multi-coloured rug on the floor, occupied by baby Ophelia kicking her legs. Colourful cushions, red predominating, decorated the brown leather sofa. Emma wasn't sure the room, or its main occupant, were in quite good taste.

"Thank you. I know from experience how difficult a time it is for you."

"I can barely hold my head up right now."

She directed Emma to an armchair, sitting herself languidly on the sofa amongst the pile of cushions. Shouts from the children penetrated as they raced past the cottage. Emma could see through the front window that Jonathan was flying a kite which the girls seemed eager to get their hands on. Emma heard the chink of crockery from the room behind.

"Put out another cup and those little orange cakes, Holly," Ruth called. Holly, that was the name of the third maid.

"Yes'm."

"Your older girls are out playing today," Emma commented.

Ruth sighed. "I tried to keep them quiet indoors as Mother Lockwood said I should, but they were bored and kept squabbling. It was really too much."

Emma nodded. "It takes time to work through grief. Getting on with life is a distraction I would recommend."

Holly appeared with the tea tray. She hesitated. There was nowhere to put it. Emma quickly moved a side table to the front of the sofa when Ruth made no attempt to help.

"May I take me break now please, Mrs. Andrew?" Holly asked after settling the tray.

Ruth frowned but told her to run along. The girl promptly slipped out the front door. Emma imagined she would be heading for the homestead kitchen. She wouldn't have been surprised if it were her own presence that had prompted the girl to ask, hoping Ruth wouldn't refuse in front of a guest.

"Would you mind pouring Emma? Cream and three sugars. I'm exhausted."

Emma leaned over the tea table and did as asked, before putting the cup nearer the woman. She didn't bother handing it to her. Half lolling as she was, Emma doubted Ruth would be able to hold it steady to drink.

"Yes, well it isn't as if they are going to miss their father all that much, I have to admit," Ruth confided. "He had so little to do with them. So long as they kept quiet and didn't trouble him it was fine, but any upset and it would be my fault for not managing them properly. He was a very selfabsorbed man if I do say so."

Not the only one in the family then. "That must have been difficult for you."

"It was. Oh, I cared for him greatly, of course, but he didn't understand me at all," Ruth confided. "I hope you don't mind me saying these things, Emma, but it's such a relief. No one here cares."

She was sure Ruth Lockwood wouldn't need much encouragement to talk. About herself anyway.

"You can't talk to your sister?"

Ruth put her handkerchief to her eye and sniffed. "Naomi doesn't speak to me. She has been horrid to me ever since I married Andrew. She is jealous, you see. She felt she should have had the eldest son, but Andrew preferred me."

"I am sorry to hear that. I'm sure she wouldn't be wishing herself in your place right now. She must be feeling very sorry for your situation."

"You are blessed if you have sisters like that, Emma. I have no one." She sniffed and raised the handkerchief to her eyes again."

"Well, you have your children," Emma said, struggling to feel some sympathy for the self-absorbed woman. "And all the Lockwood family. That must be some comfort to you. They are sharing your grief."

Ruth just shook her head. Emma was doing her best, but the more Ruth spoke the less she could credit the woman with anything except wanting attention.

"What do you think happened at the mill?" Emma ventured to ask, reaching for a cupcake as if the question was just by the by.

"Oh, it was that Irishman, wasn't it? I hear he was let go from his previous place. People don't get let go for nothing, do they? Of course, it wouldn't surprise me if Naomi did it out of spite."

"Really?" Emma almost dropped her cupcake in surprise and was sure she didn't hide her incredulity at the statement.

"You don't know her as I do, Emma," Ruth said sharply. "She is capable of anything where I am concerned." Her voice rose. "Andrew never believed me either." She thumped her hand on the edge of the sofa. "I suspect she was worming her way into his affections behind my back."

Emma was saved from responding by the front door opening noisily to admit the girls.

"Kate had a hold of the kite and she wouldn't let me have a turn," Margaret wailed.

Ophelia started at the sound and began to cry.

"You would've let it go and Jonathan would've been cross if you'd lost it," Katherine retorted. "You're just a baby."

"I am not. Fee is the baby."

"Stop it, stop it," Ruth cried putting her hands over her ears. "Katherine run and fetch Holly. Quickly now."

Katherine rolled her eyes but left to do as she was told. Ruth then ordered Margaret to her room for a rest and the girl stomped off. As Ruth sat with her head in her hands, Emma picked up Ophelia and walked about the room, rocking the baby until she quietened.

"I can't stand the noise," Ruth said looking up when Ophelia was quiet. "I'm not sorry I won't be having any more children. No more crying babies. But that's why she did it, you know. Naomi. So I couldn't have a son. She has two, and Jonathan will inherit River Bend now. That's why she killed Andrew."

EMMA WAS in a daze after her visit to Ruth. She had stayed until Holly returned and took charge of Ophelia. Little wonder the girl took the opportunity for a few minutes off when it presented itself. Emma wanted to talk to Naomi now to get her story. Would she prove as unsettling as her sister?

She set her steps toward the second cottage and saw Lieutenant Forrester coming toward her from the direction of the O'Neill's home.

"Mrs. Berry," he said as he came up to her. "Do you have any news for me?"

"I haven't spoken to everyone yet, Lieutenant," she said more snappily than she intended. He raised his eyebrows which annoyed her further. "I can't order them to speak to me, can I? At least what I do learn should be more reliable, as it is freely given." The Lieutenant frowned. Had she struck a chord? Was he having trouble getting useful answers to his questions?

She shook her head. "I'm sorry, Lieutenant. Please excuse me. I've just spoken to Ruth Lockwood and that's an experience I don't care to repeat. I was about to visit her sister and hopefully find some balance."

"Good afternoon," said a voice from behind them. Janet Felling stopped beside Emma, a bundle of folded clothes in her arms. "How are you, Lieutenant? Getting on with it, then?"

"Hello Janet," Emma said, not waiting for the Lieutenant to answer that highly suggestive query. "What do you have there?"

"Darning and patching for our Mrs. Declan," she said. "Just a nice time for a chat and a cuppa."

"Well, don't let us keep you."

"I'll see you at supper tonight, hen," Janet said and winked. Emma watched as Gladys let her into Naomi's cottage before turning back to the Lieutenant.

"Well, clearly I won't be speaking to Naomi Lock-wood right now. Possibly not until tomorrow. Could we share what we have learned to date?"

"Very well, if you've anything to offer," he said. "The farm office has been put at my disposal."

They entered the homestead at the back door and Lieutenant Forrester had Emma precede him through the vestibule, across the dining room and the main hall, and through the drawing room to the enclosed space on the side verandah, which housed the farm office. The overcast sky of the morning had passed without any more rain and the sun, low in the sky, made the room bright and warm.

It was typical of a farm office, where the paper-work was done because it had to be rather than because anyone thought it a room that needed any special comforts. Several bookcases stuffed with folders, a large desk and one other chair were enough for the purpose. Several piles of folders, probably normally on the desk, were on the floor beside a door in the outer wall. The only item on the desk, other than the Lieutenant's notebook which he now opened, was a blackened arrowhead with a burnt bit of shaft and a scrap of wire attached.

The Lieutenant seated himself behind the desk and Emma took the other chair. She felt as if she were reporting to him. In an effort to equalize the relation-ship, she spoke first.

"So, have all the men been accounted for?"

"After a fashion," the Lieutenant said glancing at his notebook.

"What does that mean, exactly?"

He turned a page not looking at her. "Where were you when the mill exploded.

"I was sitting on the bench outside Deelie's cottage. Deelie and the children were with me, as was Ruth Lockwood. I have already told you that."

He turned several more pages. "You will no doubt support one another in that statement, I imagine." Emma was about to suggest he question the children as well if he doubted her but decided it wouldn't help to irritate him when she wanted co-operation.

"So, who have you spoken to today?" he asked.

"Brendan, Ian, and Ruth Lockwood."

"And?"

"And what?"

His attention was finally drawn from his notebook as he stared at her.

"What do they have to say for themselves?" he asked. "I already know where Ian Lockwood and O'Neill were. Have they anything else to add?"

"I didn't realise I was coming here just to answer questions. I thought we were going to share information."

"That isn't the way I work. I ask questions, you answer."

"Well, I'm sorry," Emma said getting to her feet, "but that isn't the way I work. We need to put our heads together, compare what we know. If there is an arrest to be made it will be yours. Your honour for any capture. I'm not looking to claim anything. I just don't want to see the wrong person suspected, or worse still, charged."

His moustache bristled. "You think I'm afraid of missing out on the glory of solving this case?"

Emma shrugged. "I thought we had an understanding. But if you can't share information, neither can I. I will just have to solve this myself."

"You want an understanding?" he said leaning forward in his chair. "But you didn't tell me your friend O'Neill could use a bow. That he'd been taught by young Ian Lockwood. You did know that didn't you?"

He sounded just like Daniel when he told her he knew of her deal with boat builder Knowles. She refused to feel guilty.

"And you," she responded, putting her hands on his desk and looking him in he eye, "made it clear you didn't want me telling you how to run your investigation. So, I let you do it." It was a poor excuse, but she didn't care. "Besides, it hardly matters. Apparently, you can't live here without getting involved in archery." Emma hadn't seen a man splutter before. It wasn't a particularly elucidating sight. "I gather you haven't had a particularly good day," she said, stepping back from the desk and sitting down again.

He leaned back in his chair and stared up at the ceiling. Was he counting to ten, as her grandmother had often told her to do when she was a child and her brothers had irritated her?

"Is there anything else you haven't told me?" he asked finally, fixing her with a challenging eye.

Emma crossed her fingers, her hand hidden in the folds of her skirt.

"Not that I can think of," she said. With any luck he would never learn about the gate in the fence beside her friend's cottage. At least not until Brendan was no longer a suspect.

Wait. Hadn't he said he knew where Brendan was when the mill exploded?

Chapter 16

Bearding the Lieutenant

"Brendan has an alibi?"

"Of sorts."

"What does that mean? Where did he say he was?" Whatever it was, it seemed to be making the Lieutenant slightly uncomfortable too.

"He, ah..." Emma's mind raced. Brendan had been having an affair. Barbara, perhaps, or Ann. She could never tell Deelie. It would break her heart. "He was in the, ah, outhouse, at the time."

"The outhouse? At the cottage?" But he couldn't have come back to the cottage. They would have seen him, sitting out as they were. Unless he had sneaked around through the backyard.

But he couldn't have done that either. They had a view of the gate near the schoolhouse. Had he come up along the river and through the gate beside the cottage? The gate that didn't squeak? But that put him near the scene at the time of the explosion.

"No, he was referring to the outhouse behind the barn."

"Oh." She breathed a sigh of relief. It must be one of the lean-to's she had seen there.

"Apparently that's used specifically by the men. Unfortunately, no one can vouch for him and according to Frank Lockwood, O'Neill was away for a good fifteen minutes."

Brendan had said he and Frank were working on horse leathers in the stable. No wonder Frank was accusing him if he knew Brendan was missing from his assigned place during the critical minutes.

"Perhaps Brendan was somewhere else for part of those fifteen minutes. Perhaps he stopped to talk to someone, and they've forgotten, or you haven't spoken to them yet. Perhaps Frank is wrong about the time he took."

"Oh, he has an excuse. Says he was reading while he was there and got absorbed in his book, *Tom Brown's Schooldays* lent him by Ian Lockwood. He did show me the book this afternoon but that doesn't mean he had it with him at the time."

Well, it made sense to her, if not the Lieutenant. "He could have been. Ian lends him books because he's teaching Brendan to read and write." She told him what Brendan had said about improving his reading and writing skills so he could get better employment and leave River Bend and Jack Brighten behind. "That's how he was dealing with the situation with the miller. He kept out of the man's way as much as possible and concentrated on his books."

The Lieutenant considered this but didn't look convinced. "It's possible, I suppose. He's still under suspicion until someone can fill in those missing minutes. He could have slipped across to the river. It would be only a few steps then along to below the mill, do the deed, throw everything in the river, slip back up and join everyone at the mill. I timed it. Less than 5 minutes."

"I see."

"So, did you learn anything from Ruth Lockwood?"

Emma told him of their conversation. "Ruth even claimed Naomi may have done it to prevent Andrew having a son." Lieutenant Forrester raised his eyebrows at that. "It's plausible, I suppose. You would have to look at Xavier Lockwood's will to be clear on that. Is it the eldest grandson, or the eldest son of the eldest son that inherits River Bend?" The Lieutenant made a note.

"It would be a good idea to check River Bend's financial situation as well," Emma went on. "Given that Frank was throwing out accusations about at least one of his brothers wanting money for their own project, it would be interesting to know if Andrew had the funds but wouldn't spend them. Perhaps someone thought Declan might be more amenable to their requests."

The Lieutenant looked at the piles of folders on the floor. "It is on my list of the many things I need to do."

"Of course. Before we leave Ruth Lockwood, can anyone vouch for Evan's whereabouts at the time?" Emma asked.

"Evan Lockwood does not have a sound alibi," the Lieutenant admitted. "He claims he was down at his vineyard and rushed back when he heard the explosion and saw the fire. He was certainly there at some point not long after. But he could just as easily have slipped back up along the river and done the deed."

"I didn't see him, but then I couldn't be sure of telling one brother from the other at that time. I only got to see them up close briefly during the wake, but I got a better idea of them when they were installing the memorial millstone." But she was sure it was Evan visiting Ruth, and not Harold. The Lieutenant was drumming his fingers on the desk, lost in thought. "Did your troopers find anything?"

"No, and the ground had been churned up too much to show anything of use. One needs to be on hand immediately after a death like this and we had it down as an accident initially."

"Everyone had, except Frank Lockwood." Something Frank had said niggled at her. Something about Andrew not being that careless. And yet there had already been one fire. She shook it off. "This could have been planned or spur of the moment," she mused.

"Well, not so much spur of the moment, I wouldn't have thought. Someone didn't just grab up a bow and arrow and fire makings and shoot. No one was seen walking about with the weapon. I expect it was hidden, ready when needed. If anyone did it at all. I mean, I am holding off my disbelief at the moment, you understand?"

Emma nodded. She knew which way the Lieutenant was leaning. She didn't particularly care about the outcome, so long as it was clear cut with no ambiguities and Brendan no longer under suspicion.

"Evan Lockwood could have taken what he needed with him," the Lieutenant went on. "No one would have noticed."

"What about the other brothers? If Brendan wasn't with Frank for fifteen minutes, does that mean Frank was alone during that time as well?"

"He was. But he raised the suspicion that the explosion wasn't an accident. He would hardly do that if he had been responsible for it."

"Sounds like a clever way of covering himself in case anyone else became suspicious," she insisted, playing devil's advocate. "I saw Frank running from behind the barn after I got to the front of the homestead. He could as easily have just come up from the river as from the stable."

"Everyone says he idolised his brother," the Lieutenant countered.

"A matter of extremes? The more you love, the more you can hate. Perhaps Andrew did something that toppled him off that pedestal."

"Can you see that?"

Emma wasn't sure. Frank's grief seemed real enough to her. Then again, he could just be regretting his action if he had done it in the heat of the moment. But no, that wouldn't work. Frank carried his heart on his sleeve for all to see. If he had been offside with Andrew it would have been known. But not by her. She hadn't met him before the mill exploded. Something else she needed to explore.

"Ian Lockwood said you had spoken to him," Emma said. "He visited with Brendan early this afternoon."

"I spoke to him again when he was with O'Neill. He confirms lending O'Neill the book, anyway. Barbara Lockwood told me Ian was sitting at his easel when the explosion occurred, so he is ruled out."

"She saw him, did she?" He nodded. "What about Mrs. Lockwood? I imagine she was one of the first people you spoke to."

"Oh, yes."

Emma couldn't help but smile a little. He sounded quite putout. "Nothing useful there then?"

The Lieutenant patted his notebook. "Pages of 'my boys couldn't possibly have done this, it's a tragic accident, that arrow could have been lying there forever,' etcetera, etcetera. If she does know anything, or suspects something, I am never going to hear about it. She did agree to my searching the homestead, for what it was worth."

"You have been busy. I take it you found nothing to incriminate anyone?"

"On the contrary. I found too much for it to mean anything. Paraffin, rags for cleaning, even several arrowheads. Apparently, the blacksmith had made a batch of them for a special event some time back."

"Possibly for Mrs. Lockwood's birthday last year," Emma said. "I imagine the barn is full of the same things you found in the homestead."

"Including a nice collection of bows in several sizes and weights and five quivers with arrows. No shortage of the weapon."

"So, it comes down to opportunity, then." Emma ticked off on her fingers. "I was with Deelie and Ruth. Naomi and the maid, Holly, ran out of the cottages. Mrs. Fowler, Mrs. Lockwood and Barbara were at the front of the homestead when I got there. No one could possibly suspect Mrs. Lockwood, anyway.

"I saw Ann Russell in the bucket line," Emma continued. "She would have been in the schoolhouse with the children when the explosion occurred so she may have taken a few minutes to get to the front of the homestead, given the need to look after her charges. It really only leaves the men." Including Brendan.

"There are also the other two maids," Lieutenant Forrester reminded her. "But I've spoken to them all. They are all clear on where they were at the time. Not completely checked yet, but I can't see any of them being involved. Doubtful they could use a bow."

"Gladys can, of the three maids, according to Ian. What about the rest of the men? Is there anyone else you can rule out?"

Lieutenant Forrester leafed through his notebook. "Declan was here in the office. That's confirmed again by Mrs. Fowler and Barbara Lockwood. Harold was in the yard behind the cottages, talking to one of the maids. I haven't confirmed that with the maid yet."

"That would be Gladys I believe. I think she works at Naomi's cottage." The Lieutenant confirmed that Harold had said it was Gladys he was speaking with.

"I didn't see her run out of the cottage with Naomi. Perhaps she was behind me. That leaves Harold to be confirmed by Gladys, and Frank, Evan, and Brendan."

"You're still including Frank Lockwood?"

"If you include Brendan you have to include Frank." He shrugged. "What if we can't clear everyone? What if at the end of the investigation, we still have people we can't say conclusively couldn't have done it? What then?"

"I'll worry about that when we get there. The worst that could happen is no one will be charged because there isn't enough evidence pointing to anyone in particular. Which means it will come down as an accident. Which, of course," he said giving her a straight look, "it most likely is. I'm not convinced this was deliberate. What are you planning on doing now?"

"I will speak to Naomi Lockwood, Mrs. Fowler, and Barbara Lockwood. I might catch Naomi today if she's alone, and tonight I can speak to Janet Felling. I spoke to Ann Russell after the arrowhead had been found but I'll speak to her again. She might have something useful to add. She seems to know most of what's going on about the place. And you?"

"I'm going to re-interview everyone to clarify what I've found out from others. Also, I haven't spoken to the men building the new mill. And then there are the station hands employed on the property. Their quarters are some distance off toward the sheep pastures. They were out at work when I called there earlier this afternoon, so I'll catch them first thing in the morning. I don't see much possibility there, though."

Emma hoped he was right. The more people they could clear the better. Having too many possibilities left room for speculation when what Brendan needed was certainty.

Chapter 17

Naomi's Story

EVAN LOCKWOOD, his brow furrowed, was walking toward her as Emma went out the back door of the homestead. Ruth Lockwood was just closing the front door of her cottage.

"Mr. Lockwood," Emma greeted him.

He started and looked decidedly uncomfortable when he saw who had spoken.

"Mrs. Berry."

Was he worried because she had seen him coming out of Ruth's cottage? But anyone could have. He had the same blue-grey eyes as most of his siblings. His long face would have looked more attractive truncated by a beard.

"I haven't had a chance to speak to you before," Emma said. "Please accept my condolences on the death of your brother. It's a sad time for your family."

Evan nodded, a shadow passing over his face. "Thank you. We're going to miss him."

There seemed little else to say on that. Asking what he thought had caused the fire seemed to be out of place. He was about to move on when Alfie came racing over from where he had been hanging about with the children, Jonathan still flying his kite. Emma bent and scratched the dog's head. He sat back and looked up at her.

"Seems to have taken to you," Evan said bending to give the dog a pat. "He's a real scamp. Always getting into mischief. I've seen him climb this fence to get out, you know."

"Has he now." Emma looked at the wire mesh fence. She could imagine Alfie doing that. Beagles were real escape artists.

"Yeah. Never bothers to climb back in, though."

Emma laughed. Did she see the curtain twitch in Ruth's front window? She decided to try a direct request to get time to talk to him.

"I would love to see your vineyard before I leave, Mr. Lockwood, and I leave on Thursday. Could you show me over it tomorrow? I would really appreciate it. My father would be most interested to hear about your efforts." Her father had never expressed such a thing, but Evan needn't know that.

"Oh, right." He was looking uncomfortable again. "Are you sure you wouldn't prefer to spend the time with your friends?"

"Perhaps Deelie O'Neill could come with me."

"Oh, ah, yes, of course."

"What time would you want to go?"

"Ah, nine o'clock? Meet you out the front. I'll have the buggy ready." He was easing his way toward the back door.

"I look forward to it."

She reminded herself to get some treats for Alfie. He was proving most helpful when it came to introductions. First Ian, and now Evan.

There was still time to speak to Naomi Lockwood before supper. She approached the front door of her cottage hoping this time to find her alone. The maid Gladys opened the door to her knock and directed Emma to the kitchen where she found Naomi putting the finishing touches to a casserole. A cake sat cooling on a rack on the table and the woman's round face was flushed. She looked a little startled at Emma's sudden appearance.

"I hope I'm not intruding," Emma said. "Gladys let me in and just pointed in this direction."

Naomi shook her head. "Oh, that girl. She's in a daydream most of the time. Completely wrapped up in one of my brothers-in-law."

"Oh, which one?"

"Harold." Naomi rolled her eyes. "Young love. What can I do for you?"

"I couldn't leave without calling in to see how you are doing after this terribly sad event."

"That's very thoughtful of you," Naomi said. "Let me get this food on cooking and we can have a cuppa and cake, and a nice chat. Please, take a seat." She indicated a place at the kitchen table and Emma was happy to comply.

Naomi put the casserole dish in the oven, and picked up the kettle, which was singing gently on the hob. Emma was surprised to see her doing for herself instead of having Gladys make the tea. Whatever airs Ruth liked to put on, her sister clearly had a far more down to earth approach.

"How are you doing?" Emma asked when they had tea and cakes in front of them.

"I have to admit to feeling quite flat," Naomi admitted. "I am keeping busy in the hope of passing the time without thinking too much."

"Is it helping?"

"Not entirely." Emma nodded in sympathy and sipped her tea. "You're a friend of that policeman, aren't you? We were talking about you at lunch. Someone saw you talking to him on the track on his way in this morning."

Ann. Couldn't wait to tell everyone. Naomi looked at her expectantly.

"I wouldn't call myself a friend, exactly," Emma said. "I met him last year in an official capacity. He was stationed at Euston at the time."

"But anything you hear you are going to pass on to him, aren't you?"

"Not everything, no. Just what will help discover who fired that arrow into the mill. If someone did, of course. You would like that matter settled I imagine?"

Naomi shivered. "Not if it turns out to be one of the family. You don't believe it was the Irishman? Of course, you wouldn't," she added, answering her own question. "They're friends of yours. It still could be him, though, couldn't it?"

Emma had no answer to that. Brendan's alibi was still in the wind.

"It seems a rather outlandish thing to do just to get back at the miller's nasty comments, though, wouldn't you say?" she asked instead. Naomi shrugged. "Did anyone else have a problem with Jack Brighten?"

"I never had anything to do with him. As far as I know, no one in the family did except Andrew. He was just an employee, even if a specialist." She sipped her tea.

"I was speaking to Ruth earlier. I don't think the reality of her husband's death has hit her yet."

Naomi's laugh startled her. "Oh, Ruth's reality is of her own making." She sobered. "She has been the bane of my life since our mother died. I was eleven and Ruth was only six years old. Mother had been ill for some time, and I had to take over the household and become mother to my sister. Fortunately, I'd already had some schooling and I've always read so I wasn't giving up anything to take over the household. But Ruth resented it from the start. It was a constant battle between the two of us. I won't boor you with the details." Naomi heaved a sigh. "And then Andrew began courting me."

"How did your father feel about that? He must have been reliant on you?" Emma prompted as Naomi seemed to be lost in memories for a moment.

"Father encouraged it. He thought I was making a good match and he was proud of it. He thought Ruth should take over the housekeeping for him until it was her turn to marry, but Ruth didn't like the idea. I felt responsible for them both. My cross to bear. I decided that if Ruth married first and was off our hands, I would then be free to marry at my leisure. But Andy didn't want to wait. He liked his own way and could be stiff necked." She sighed and shook her head. Emma could well imagine it.

"Declan had started visiting along with Andy by then," Naomi went on, "and he was showing some interest in Ruth, but still Andy wouldn't back down. Ruth suggested we could have a double wedding, but then Declan didn't seem to be in any hurry to declare himself. It was a stand-off." Naomi crumbled the remaining piece of her cake into tiny pieces. "I don't know if he and Andrew discussed it, I've never asked, but Andrew decided to marry Ruth instead."

"Oh, dear."

Naomi nodded. "Yes, and then Declan proposed to me. He said it was always me he preferred, and he couldn't imagine why Andy would choose Ruth. I think he and I were both lucky as it turned out."

"Did that cause problems between Andrew and Declan?"

"Oh, they were fine for the most part. Declan didn't argue with Andy. He would find ways to make Andy's ideas work for everyone. Except for the mill. Dec didn't think the mill was a good idea, but Father Lockwood was still in charge when it was built, and he was the type of person who, if you told him something wasn't a good idea, would immediately go ahead with it." It seemed Ian's painting of his father didn't lie then.

"Were there any issues about the children? I mean, the fact you have boys and Andrew didn't have a son. Yet anyway."

"I'll warrant that idea came from Ruth," Naomi said shrewdly. "Andy would have had a son eventually, and he would have been the one to inherit. Eldest son of eldest son. But our Jonathan will be the heir now."

"That is the way it's usually done with landed families," Emma agreed. Which meant Declan and Naomi had a motive but they also both had alibis.

"Unfair as it seems to the younger brothers. But my father-in-law wanted to make sure the farm survived intact. It was up to Andrew to decide what help the other boys received, depending on the finances of the property.

"I have to say, Andy has tried his best to increase the farm revenue. The problem is that this land can't support a large number of sheep. Apparently, when Father Lockwood selected it, there had been a great flood, and the land was green with lush pastures, lightly treed. Perfect for grazing. As you know Emma, in between the floods are years and years of little rain and sometimes drought."

Emma did know. He wouldn't have been the first to make that mistake. "Was your husband happy with his particular role on the property?"

Naomi laughed. "Do you mean was he waiting for a share, so he could move on?"

"I'm sorry. It's not really my business but understanding the people and their circumstances will help the Lieutenant in his investigation," Emma said apologetically.

"It's quite all right. I don't mind you asking these things. It isn't a secret. No, Declan has made his place here. Andrew is – was – oh dear." She paused. "He was always looking to the future. He was too impatient with the bookwork and small details. Declan took care of all that and was happy to do so. He tended to act as a buffer between Andrew and the younger boys as much as possible. Andrew could be difficult to talk to." She nodded. "They actually made a surprisingly good team. I hope Declan won't feel too overwhelmed with everything now."

"Did Andrew spend a lot of time in the mill?" Emma realised that had been bothering her for some time. Surely it was something for an employee or a younger brother to take on while Andrew concentrated on the bigger issues. Was it her imagination or did Naomi look a little uncertain at the question? If so, she recovered quickly.

"Oh, yes," she said. "It was his special project. And with the trouble between the miller and your friend, he didn't want them working together."

That didn't answer why one of the brothers couldn't have worked there. Was she missing something?

"I hope Ruth will be all right," Emma said. "She seems to be close to Ann Russell."

"Ann panders to her. She likes that."

Emma was taking her leave when she remembered Harold's alibi.

"Was Gladys here when the mill exploded?"

"She's here most of the time, and it was wash day, so yes."

"Was anyone else around?"

Naomi shook her head. "Not that I noticed. No one had visited. It was still early."

Emma thanked her again for speaking with her, and Naomi saw her out. It had been an interesting and pleasant conversation, but Emma wasn't sure it had added anything useful.

Chapter 18

Deelie & Brendan at Odds

"I SAW YON Emma talking to that Lieutenant again today," Janet announced, as she helped Deelie serve up the last of Mrs. Fowlers casseroles, lamb this time. Emma, who had taken a seat at the table with Liam on her lap, wasn't sure how she felt about being referred to as if she weren't there. "He's a tidy one. I ken not all their talk is about this business."

"Emma has more lovers than anyone I know," Deelie said. "Evan is taking her to see his vineyard tomorrow."

"Oh, aye?"

"I'm investigating this business, as you call it, Janet. People will tell me things they won't tell the Lieutenant."

"But hasn't the Lieutenant already questioned Evan?" Janet wanted to know.

"He has. But Evan had gone down to the vineyard which gave him the opportunity to slip back up along the river and fire the arrow. He didn't appear until later. Has there ever been any suggestions of something between him and Ruth?"

"Ruth and Mr. Evan?" Deelie repeated. "Heaven above, no. Why would you think that?"

"I saw Evan come out the back door of Ruth's cottage that night, the day the mill exploded, just as I was getting ready for bed."

"The back door?"

"Yes."

"That doesn't look good, does it? But he's nice, Evan is. I've seen him with the children sometimes. He'll stop and talk to them, and they'll be smiling and talking back. I never saw Mr. Andrew do that, not even to his own girls, and they never went to him. It'll be Mrs. Andrew pulling Mr. Evan I'm thinking, and he being too nice to say no to her."

"Oh, aye. She likes to be admired that one," Janet put in.

"That's a sad situation between Ruth and Naomi," Emma said. "Perhaps now that Andrew is gone, they may be able to patch up their differences."

"You don't suspect them of shooting that arrow do you, hen?"

"I suspect everyone until I know otherwise, but they both have alibis." Liam went to grab at the plate Janet placed in front of her. "Hold on. It's a little hot for you yet." Deelie gave her a small plate and she spooned some lamb and vegetables on it to cool. It smelled delicious.

"Rory and meself, as well then?" Janet asked.

"Oh, aye," Emma said mimicking her. "Where were you when the mill exploded?"

"Mixing up a batch of scones. What a waste. Had to throw it out when I finally got back. Just as well they weren't in the oven, is all I can say. They would have been burnt to a crisp."

She put her hand to her mouth as soon as the words were out. No one spoke for a moment as they tried not to conjure up the image of what had taken place in the mill.

"The explosion would have done for them at once," Rory said. It was what everyone wanted to believe.

Emma decided against asking any more questions tonight about who had seen what. She spooned food into Liam's waiting mouth and managed another forkful for herself.

Janet, however, needed to talk. "Ian was lying on the ground and Rory scrambling to get to him. Everyone was running out from the homestead, from everywhere. Mr. Declan, Mr. Harold, I saw them."

"You were in the bucket line, weren't you?" Emma asked. Janet nodded. "Who was near you?"

"Mrs. Fowler and Ann were right next."

Emma nodded and looked to Rory.

"I already know you all saw me," he said. "I saw the mill explode, pieces going everywhere. I saw Ian get knocked down and I came right away out of the smithy. I told the Lieutenant."

"You were at the end of the bucket chain, filling the buckets," Emma said, remembering what she had seen afterward, his boots and trousers wet past his knees as he carried Ian indoors. A handy man to have about the place.

Janet was looking thoughtful as they finished their dessert. "Do you think it wise to be going off with yon Evan on your own tomorrow, hen?" she asked.

Deelie looked alarmed. "Ooh, yes. You should take someone with you, Emma."

Emma realised she hadn't asked Deelie if she would accompany her. She'd only suggested it to Evan on the spur of the moment when he was hesitating. It probably wouldn't be convenient anyway, with Orla needing Deelie's attention.

"I'll go," Brendan offered.

"It should be a woman," Emma said. Two men together. She wouldn't get to talk to Evan the way she needed to. "And you're still confined to home, anyway."

Janet and Deelie looked at one another.

"It might look odd, me going," Janet said apologetically, "as you're here to visit with Deelie. How about I look after the bairns and Deelie goes with you?"

"I haven't seen the vineyard," Deelie said, "so Mr. Evan wouldn't be surprised if I was there."

Brendan frowned. "Don't I get a say on it?"

"Emma is trying to help us, Bren. We're not for putting her in danger. What can he do with the two of us and everyone knowing where we are?" Deelie argued.

"What if we give you an hour, and then me and Bren come walking down," Janet suggested. "Just in case."

"And why would you be doing that, wife?" Rory asked.

"I can't think of anything I'd rather do than take a quiet walk with a handsome Irishman, now," Janet teased.

"You'll set tongues wagging," Deelie said, l aughing.

"Oh, aye. And me old enough to be his ma."

"I can be looking for a good spot to put a fish trap and meet Janet on the way," Brendan said. "I'll have to walk along the river for a way though, as I'm not supposed to be out and about."

"You can't do that, anyway," Deelie said. "You'll be taking care of the children."

Janet looked crestfallen at having her rescue plan dashed. "We've not had this much excitement since the rooster got out last Christmas and chased everyone around the yard."

Emma shook her head at them. "I'm happy for Deelie to come. We'll be perfectly safe. It's not as if

I'm going to accuse Evan of killing his brother." Well, not in so many words perhaps.

It was finally decided that Janet would come over a little before nine to help Brendan with the children.

"Take something to defend yourself with, hen," Janet advised as she and Rory left.

"I don't like the idea of you going to the vineyard with Evan," Brendan said, when the three of them were alone. "Neither one of you. I'm thinking I should go along."

"You can't Bren. And there's no danger. Not from Mr. Evan."

"You seem right taken with him."

Deelie stared at him, seeming aghast at the implied accusation. Before she could respond Emma spoke up, brooking no argument.

"If this is going to cause trouble between the two of you, I will go on my own. I was intending to do that anyway until Janet started with her ideas."

"The explosion was an accident," Brendan insisted. "Anything else is madness. No one in their right mind would blow up the mill with people working inside of it."

"Then there's no danger from Mr. Evan, is there," Deelie said stoutly. "And nothing else either, Bren."

Brendan stared at her, frustration and helplessness warring on his face as Deelie, hands on hips, stared defiantly back.

Emma felt sick. She hoped she would learn something from Evan tomorrow to turn this around, before her friends' marriage became another casualty.

Chapter 19

Challenging Evan

EVAN WAS waiting for Emma next morning, with a buggy hitched and ready behind the barn. Was that a look of relief when she arrived with Deelie? There was a slight early morning chill in the air, but the sun promised some warmth if you were out of the wind and Evan had thoughtfully included several rugs. Or more likely his mother had as she came out just as they were about to leave.

Mrs. Lockwood seemed alarmed when she saw Deelie, but it turned out she had provided a picnic morning tea and there were only two cups and plates. They waited while Mrs. Fowler repacked the basket with enough for three. Janet waved to them on her way to help Brendan with the children.

"Are you warm enough?" Evan asked from his driver's seat as they trotted down the track beside the river. "I don't feel the cold so much myself."

"We're very comfortable, Mr. Lockwood, thank you."

Fifteen minutes later they were passing the first rows of the little vineyard. And little it was with only a dozen rows of trellised vines, stretching for about the length of a cricket pitch. The leaves were showing their autumn colours of yellows and browns, but in between the rows were the strips of green Emma had seen from the mill; winter peas.

"Legumes return nitrogen to the soil," Evan explained as they walked the length of the vineyard and back. Deelie walked behind them, like a good chaperone.

Evan took them to the riverbank where a wind-mill-powered pump sat, a pipe leading one way into the water and another to the first row of vines. The windmill was disconnected from the pump, only being hitched up when it was time to water.

"I can pump by hand if I need if there's no wind. See how this works?"

Evan turned a handle vigorously and Emma rushed to watch at the end of the pipe, cheering when water flowed out into the furrow. Evan was red in the face when he stopped turning. It wasn't the most efficient method.

"Have you thought of using a horseworks when there is insufficient wind? We use one at Wirramilla for the house water and the gardens."

"I would need to when the vineyard is full size," Evan said, seeming pleased at her interest. "But this is enough for the moment. I might need a dam later."

Emma agreed a dam would be a good idea for the future.

"So how was it going to work, your vineyard?" Emma asked as Deelie moved to sit on the edge of a wooden cart a few steps away. "I mean, the land isn't yours, is it? You must have some arrangement with your brother." She didn't stipulate which brother.

He looked at her quizzically. "I wouldn't have thought that was anyone else's business. Though I suppose you might be interested given the – ah – situation." So, he understood she was asking questions about the explosion. "It hadn't been decided. It would either be a lease of the land or a sharecropping agreement."

"I see." Emma fingered a yellowed vine leaf. "Did you have a preference?"

"The fairest option."

"That's perfectly reasonable. Let me guess. It would be the sharecropping."

Evan's stance relaxed a little. "Why would you choose that?" he asked as if he genuinely wanted to know.

"Well, sharecropping is based on a percentage of profits, but a land lease is a flat fee. Either would work on a good harvest – the lease might even be better at that time – but it could prove expensive if you had a poor year. Charge according to the return is fairer to both parties if the project is successful."

"Pity you weren't going to be my landlord, Mrs. Berry. Andy wanted the lease. He wasn't prepared to trust that the vineyard would be profitable."

"And your new landlord? Has he made a decision on that?"

"We haven't discussed it."

The land, however, was only part of the issue. Evan still had to get the vineyard fully planted and Andrew had been preventing that from happening. Emma didn't want to accuse Evan outright of murdering his brother for the money to advance the vineyard.

"The police are wondering if your brother died because he was preventing someone from getting what they wanted," she said.

"Meaning me because I wanted to expand the vineyard?" Evan challenged. Well, she hadn't been terribly subtle after all. "Seems to me there are other people wanting something."

"One of your brothers, you mean?"

"I wasn't referring to my brothers."

Emma frowned. "Is there someone outside the family who wanted something from Andrew?" This was a new line.

"Well, you should know," Evan muttered looking uncomfortable once again. Was she getting close to uncovering something important?

"How would I know?"

"Don't give me that." The cool look Evan flashed her now showed a close resemblance to the portrait of his father. It seemed all the Lockwood men were the same when you scratched the skin. "It's why you came here in the first place, isn't it? And now you're trying to find out if I'm worth the trouble. Just because you own a riverboat. Andy couldn't wait to get his hands on it."

Emma's mind reeled. She took a step back and felt something hard against her legs. She slumped backwards and found herself half lying across the wooden cart, almost knocking Deelie off her perch. She struggled to get upright and found herself being pulled into a sitting position, Deelie holding one arm and Evan the other.

"Are you all right?" Deelie asked.

"I really do need to sit for moment," Emma said putting a hand to her forehead. She was mortified. No wonder Andrew had taken the time to talk to her and size her up. She was being vetted as a prospective wife for Evan. She wondered if she had passed muster as a possible Lockwood.

Not that she thought the bar would be set high. So long as she didn't disgrace the family, Andrew probably didn't care, it was about what she would bring with her, her share in the *Mary B*. Ann's cryptic remarks the first time Emma had spoken to her suddenly made sense. And Ruth, warning her not to mention the vineyard to Evan. She didn't want his attention on anyone but herself.

"I believe Mrs. Fowler has provided a lovely morning tea," Deelie said to Evan. "It would be a pity for it to go to waste. A nice hot cup of tea would go really well about now."

Evan looked confused. Emma's reaction was likely not what he had been expecting. It was embarrassing for them both. Entertaining her to morning tea was probably the last thing he wanted to do, but he had been raised with good manners at least. He went to fetch the rug and basket from the buggy.

Emma and Deelie made to follow him toward the river when Deelie stopped, her hand going to her mouth. Emma looked to see what had caught her attention. In the cart, partly covered by a tarpaulin which Emma's fall had dislodged, was a collection of tools. Among them was a bow. Emma lifted the cover to reveal several arrows. The concerned look on Deelie's face was no doubt reflected on her own. Were they about to have morning tea with a killer?

Emma grabbed Deelie's hand and they joined Evan at a sheltered clearing on the riverbank. Ancient red gums, their branches wide and spreading, stood as if protecting the space. Across on the far side a flock of woolly merinos was gathered under another majestic red gum that commanded a space of its own. The sun filtered through the branches, while below them the river moved sluggishly.

Evan spread the rug under the trees. Deelie took charge, opening the picnic basket and pouring tea into three cups from a billy wrapped in a quilted cover. She passed around the biscuit tin inside of which was a neatly sliced apple strudel. Evan, looking as if he would rather be anywhere else than sitting on the other side of the rug, silently took a slice while Emma sought to find a way into a conversation with the man.

She took a sip of tea, both hands wrapped around the cup as she pushed down the embarrassment that surged. There were more important things at stake right now than her ego.

"I gather from what you've said, Mr. Lockwood, that there was some expectation about my visit. I want to assure you I had no knowledge of it. I came here with the sole purpose of visiting my friends, not... Was this Andrew's idea, because of my part-ownership in a riverboat?"

Evan plucked at the rug fringe. "Andy could be a little – mercenary, but Ma liked the idea too. Seems she was rather taken with you."

Emma smiled thinly. "But you were not. Which is fine," she hastened to add as Evan flushed. "Do I take it you have your eye on someone else?" He nodded. "You were coming from Ruth's cottage when I met you yesterday, Mr. Lockwood. How is she doing?"

He frowned. "She's taking it hard. As you would expect."

"She's very young still."

"Barely eighteen when she and Andy married. I suggested she go stay with her father for a bit, but she got upset. Said I was trying to be rid of her, that no one wanted her here."

"Oh, the poor girl," Emma said trying to sound sympathetic. "Still, your visits must be a comfort to her, though you must be careful she doesn't get too attached in her grief. Unless of course, that is what you want?"

Evan almost choked on his strudel. "Are you suggesting I'm interested in my brother's wife?"

"I've no idea, Mr. Lockwood. I'm just offering a friendly warning, as a sister might. Ruth may take your visits to indicate an interest you may not have."

"Oh, for the love of... A sisterly warning, you say. Well, you sound very much like Barbara, I'll give you that."

"I'm sure Barbara would tell you the same thing if she were aware of the situation. She is dealing with her own grief and may not have noticed your visits to your sister-in-law."

"And you did of course, and putting two and two together came up with…" He shook his head. "Did you think I wanted Andy out of the way, so I could claim his widow? That is unbelievable." Evan shook his head again muttering something under his breath. Emma didn't catch it but Deelie, who was sitting a little nearer, gave him a sharp look. Emma didn't think she wanted to know.

"It's none of your business," he went on. "Well, I suppose it is in a way given what Ma and Andrew were ... It's just I sort of have someone else in mind for a wife, just to set the facts straight. I'm not in a position to do anything about it yet, not until I get this vineyard up and running."

"I don't know very much about vines, I must admit, but doesn't it take several years before a vineyard is producing?"

"Three or four, yes."

Four years to wait before he could even think about marrying. No wonder he was concerned about wasting another season. Mrs. Wilson must be right in believing Evan was interested in Zoe. Encouraging him to declare himself wouldn't be a good idea if he turned out to have murdered his brother to hasten the opportunity.

"That's a shame," she said.

"It will likely be all right. Lizzie is only sixteen," Evan said, his tone softening.

"Lizzie?"

"Lizzie Ballard. She lives with her aunt and uncle, Doc Wilson and his wife. I can afford to wait a few years for her to grow up a little."

Emma popped a piece of strudel in her mouth and chewed hard to keep herself from laughing. This would be one in the eye for Mrs. Wilson and her precious Zoe.

"I know Lizzie," Emma managed to say at last. "She's a lovely girl." With some nice saleable property left her by her father for when she came of age. "Have you let Dr. Wilson know of your interest in his niece?" she asked.

"Not yet. Like I said, I can't marry yet and she's still young."

Emma remembered Ian had his eye on Lizzie too. She wondered if Andrew had known of Ian's interest and had Lizzie in mind for him, while she had been slated for Evan. Andrew had a little too much input in his brothers' lives in Emma's opinion.

Deelie poured them all a second cup of tea and offered the strudel once again. Emma's thoughts turned to the bow and arrows in the cart.

"Were you nearby when the mill exploded?" she asked Evan.

"No, I was down here, pottering about. I heard it, looked up and saw flames shooting into the sky. Couldn't believe my eyes."

"What do you think happened?"

Evan shook his head. "It was an accident. There was a small fire in the mill a couple of days before. Andy should have taken notice and been more careful."

Frank had thought so too, though he believed Andrew would have been more careful and therefore the explosion had to have been caused by something, or someone, else.

"Do you have a use for a bow and arrow down here?" Emma asked. "I see you have them in the cart. Do you use them to deter the birds?"

Evan snorted. "A flock of starlings can decimate a ripening crop. Along with many other birds."

"Mmm. I guess arrows would be a losing battle. How would you protect a large vineyard?"

"If you'd looked more closely you would have seen a roll of netting in the cart as well. That is much more effective than trying to shoot birds out of the sky." He got to his feet and walked away to stand, hands in pockets, gazing at the river. Conversation over.

Emma and Deelie packed up the morning tea leftovers and Evan drove them back to the homestead.

"You have visitors," Emma said, as they arrived at the horse paddock. Two horses were being walked about by a groom while a brougham stood nearby. Evan greeted the man. "Someone you know?"

"He works at the livery stable, but it'll be Mrs. Wilson visiting. She'll have brought her daughter and Lizzie, Miss Ballard, with her." He cast a quick glance toward the homestead. Emma imagined he was eager to join them. "Look, ah, I'm sorry if I spoke a bit rough earlier. This whole thing with Andy has got us all upset. We're not ourselves right now and... well..."

"I do understand," Emma hastened to reassure him. "By the way, once this matter has been resolved you might want to speak to Dr. Wilson. It wouldn't hurt to let him know your intentions toward Lizzie. You wouldn't want someone else to get in first, would you?" Especially his younger brother.

Evan looked a little startled as if the idea hadn't occurred to him. Emma couldn't see any reason for him to stay his hand. She doubted he'd had anything to do with his brother's death.

Chapter 20

Mrs. Fowler Has Her Say

EMMA AND DEELIE went their way by the schoolhouse gate, Deelie to her cottage and Emma to the back door of the homestead. Emma gave Deelie a hug before parting.

"Thank you for coming this morning. It definitely helped."

"You don't think he could have done it, do you?"

"I can't see it, Deelie."

"It hasn't helped Bren then, has it?" Deelie turned and walked off before Emma could answer. Not that she had anything encouraging to say. When she went to the kitchen to return the picnic basket, she found Mrs. Fowler alone.

"I see Mrs. Lockwood has guests," Emma said after greeting the woman.

"Mrs. Wilson and young Zoe and little Lizzie Ballard. Miss Barbara is with them too. I've just taken them in some morning tea. Did you enjoy your visit with Mr. Evan?"

"It was very pleasant. I will be interested to hear of the development of his vineyard. I imagine it will happen eventually, though everyone's plans might be put on hold for a time while they recover from this tragedy."

"I've no doubt. They all have their ideas, of course. Mr. Harold wants to open a store in town. Can you see him competing with Mr. Egge?"

"Well, if he gets himself a good little helpmate and chooses the right location, I don't see why not. A corner shop perhaps."

"I'm sure our Gladys would be willing enough for that," Mrs. Fowler said. "Not sure Isabel would want it, but she's going to have to let them make their own lives. And I've told her so more than once, for all she's trying to hang onto them. Can I get you a cuppa? I usually take a break about now. Breakfast's over, morning tea's been delivered, and the girls are about their work."

Emma didn't think she had room for so much as a mouthful of tea, but she might not get another such opportunity to talk to the housekeeper.

"Thank you. There's a slice of strudel left in the tin, too," she told the woman. "Why don't you have that with your tea. It was delicious, by the way."

"As I was saying," Mrs. Fowler said when they were seated at the kitchen table, tea in front of them, and her plate showing only crumbs, "I don't think it's healthy for all the boys to stay here. Men need to have control of their own lives, else there's trouble."

"Do you think that is what's happened here?"

Mrs. Fowler shook her head. "I've lived long enough, Mrs. Berry, to understand people pretty well. I simply can't see one of the boys taking down the mill in that way. But nor do I see Mr. O'Neill doing it, either."

"But someone could have."

"If you take the situation as a whole it can look that way, but when you take them individual like, one at a time, no. I can't make it fit any one of them." Mrs. Fowler licked her finger and picked up the crumbs of strudel from the plate. "If no one could have done it, it must have been an accident," she said firmly.

"That's still possible. What were you doing when the mill exploded? Who did you see?"

"Like I told that Lieutenant, I was here in my kitchen, where I always am. I thought it was the end of the world, that huge noise. Judgement Day I thought it was. I have to say I fair shook in my shoes. Not but what I've always lived a decent life, but no one is innocent altogether, are they?"

"That's certainly true," Emma said. "Tell me what you did?"

"I run out. Barbara with me. Everyone ran out from the cottages, the barn. I sent Holly back to take care of Ophelia and Norman."

"Most commendable of you, Mrs. Fowler. A cool head in an emergency. And Maudie? Where was she?"

"She was sitting in the vestibule polishing the silver. It's getting time for the family dinner they have every fortnight and Mrs. Lockwood likes the silver to be just so."

"And Gladys was hanging the wash out for Naomi. That's been confirmed."

"Good. My three little maids I call them. Though I can't see what reason they would have."

"Tell me about the boys, Mrs. Fowler. What was Mr. Andrew really like?"

"Oh, more like his father than the others, though Mr. Harold comes close. Mr. Xavier groomed Andrew to take charge, of course. He was the only boy, you see, followed by two girls. Mr. Declan is seven years younger. And Mr. Andrew, he always had his eye on the main chance." She frowned. "Like with that Jack Brighten. He came cheap because he was desperate for work. No one here would have been much concerned if he was all that got killed."

Emma thought that was certainly true, if rather sad. Frank wouldn't have gone searching for a clue as to why the mill had exploded.

"It was the same when Mr. Andrew started courting one of the Gulbis girls, whichever one you believe came first. There was the livery stable to consider."

"It will go to the girls?"

"Well, to their husbands now. I mean, to Mr. Declan, anyway. Tom Gulbis only has his daughters. The family may sell it off of course, but the money will be useful no doubt. Mr. Andrew, he certainly wouldn't look at a girl unless she had something, no matter how pretty her face and manners. But that's only right. A girl should have a dowry. Did you know in some places like Africa the man pays the father for the girl? I read about it in the *Sketcher*. It's all back to front, but what you would expect from natives I suppose. All I had when I married Mr. Fowler, rest his soul, was some good linen but that was our lot back then."

Emma didn't think it would be wise to disagree, but a society that accepted a woman as valuable and needing to be paid for, rather than a burden who had to bring something of monetary value with her, did have appeal.

"I'm a little puzzled. If Mr. Harold is interested in Gladys how would Mr. Andrew have felt about that? Gladys doesn't have anything to bring to the family except herself, does she?"

"Ah, see that's what I mean about Mr. Harold being like his brother," she tapped the side of her head. "If they weren't living here at River Bend, Mr. Andrew wouldn't have the say, and you can be sure Mr. Harold would have sold him the idea of the family owning a shop and how someone like Gladys was the perfect wife for such a venture." Emma thought Mrs. Fowler was no slouch herself when it came to being smart.

"And Mr. Declan?"

"If I have any favourite its him. And Mr. Evan," Mrs. Fowler said smiling. "Those two have always been in Mr. Andrew's shadow, Mr. Declan especially. Mr. Declan now, he'll talk to his brothers more about the running of the place. I wouldn't be surprised if he does some of that peppercorn rent business for Mr. Evan's vineyard. It's not as if that land is needed for anything else. He'll have the final say, for certain, but he'll listen and try to consider what they want and what is fair."

"And what about Mr. Evan?"

Mrs. Fowler looked at her shrewdly. "Well, you've just spent some time with him, Mrs. Berry. What did you see?"

What indeed? She didn't want to influence Mrs. Fowler's thoughts. "He's concerned about the future of his vineyard and he has his eye on Lizzie Ballard. Apart from that, I don't think our acquaintance was of sufficient length to say much more."

"Lizzie Ballard, eh?" She wagged her finger knowingly. "I didn't believe it was that Zoe Wilson he was after." She chuckled. Not a fan of the Wilson women either then.

"He's concerned about Ruth. She seems to want his company quite a lot."

"Ah, latched onto Mr. Evan, has she? Thought I saw him going to her cottage yesterday." Mrs. Fowler patted Emma's hand. "Isabel will soon put a stop to anything going on there. Miss Ruth had Mr. Andrew wrapped around her little finger when he married her, but he soon found he hadn't got such a good bargain there. And then when Mr. Declan married her sister, well, he realised his brother had done the better."

"Did Mr. Harold or Mr. Evan argue with Mr. Andrew about the money they needed for their projects?"

"They didn't argue any more than anyone else, Mrs. Berry. Mr. Harold is only twenty two. He's got lots of years ahead of him yet." So had Andrew until a few days ago. "But it isn't going to make any difference who's in charge. If the money wasn't there for these things before it still isn't going to be there now."

Unless there was insurance. The thought popped into Emma's mind as she remembered the newspaper articles on the South Australian Insurance Company and all those burning flour mills. Could insurance money be behind this somehow? Was there some sort of conspiracy among some of the brothers? Or was Andrew himself involved? That made more sense.

"Mrs. Berry? Are you feeling all right?"

"Oh, yes. Just had a thought, that's all. Tell me, did Mr. Frank want anything?"

"He looks after the horses and the carts and all. Nothing that puts too much strain on him, you understand. He had no plans to leave as I ever heard, and I can't see as he ever would. He's never got over Georgia dying. She was his twin, you know. She died from the measles when they were nine."

Mrs. Fowler's eyes misted. She took off her spectacles and rubbed them with the corner of her apron.

"Such a lovely girl," she said, putting the glasses back on. "Frank had the measles too, but he recovered, and after that he just latched onto Mr. Andrew. Like a limpet he was. Why Mr. Andrew and not one of the other boys or Barbara or Clarissa, I have no idea. Nor what he'll do now. Start to think for himself one can only hope. He and Miss Ann looked like they might be interested in one another for a while, but that seems to have come to nothing."

"He and Mr. Andrew hadn't had a falling out recently, had they?"

Mrs. Fowler gave her an odd look.

"Funny you should say that. I did hear them arguing about a week ago. Well, not arguing so much as Mr. Frank asking for something and Mr. Andrew refusing and then Mr. Frank saying he would keep asking."

"And you don't know what it was about?"

"Oh, likely something he wanted for the stable, or a new lamp for the brougham, something like that. It usually was."

"So, what about Mr. Ian. Oh, and I almost forgot Barbara."

"Almost everyone forgets Miss Barbara," Mrs. Fowler remarked drily.

"She seems a nice person."

"Oh, she is. But she doesn't do anything with herself, her appearance I mean. It's not natural I'm sure, but with all these brothers she decided years ago she wasn't ever going to marry."

"She wants to look after them, does she?"

"Oh, no. She doesn't want a man running her life. Says she's had enough of that already." Emma thought of her own life and couldn't hold that against her.

"And Mr. Ian?"

"His mother's favourite." Mrs. Fowler wagged her finger at Emma as if in warning. "The baby of the family often is. Sometimes means they keep getting treated like a baby too, and not allowed to grow up properly. Remember that. Isabel does spoil him over this painting lark but there's no doubt he has a talent. That portrait of Mr. Xavier hanging over the dining table, have you seen that?" Emma nodded. "That's him to a T."

Mrs. Fowler collected up their empty teacups. Emma was about to leave and report to the Lieutenant on her latest findings when she remembered Alfie.

"Mrs. Fowler, do you have any dog treats? I'd really like to give Alfie something when he behaves himself. Sort of an encouragement."

"Oh, well there's some pieces of beef jerky Isabel gives Beauty occasionally. You could have a few of those, I suppose." She produced a tin from a drawer and proceeded to wrap a few pieces in waxed paper.

"Thank you. I'm sure Alfie will say thank you too. It's been pleasant talking to you Mrs. Fowler."

Emma desperately wanted to talk to Lieutenant Forrester. She needed to sound him out on her insurance theory, although how you proved it and still removed suspicion from anyone, she had no idea.

Chapter 21

The Family Plays Its Hand

EMMA HEADED toward the farm office to find the Lieutenant, taking, without thinking, the same route he had taken her the day before, through the dining room and across the hall. She stepped confidently into the drawing room. And stopped. She had forgotten Mrs. Lockwood had visitors. Embarrassment brought a hot flush to her face, her hand to her throat.

"Oh, I am sorry. I didn't realise – how rude of me."

Six startled faces stared back at her. Mrs. Lockwood and Barbara were sitting on a sofa facing Mrs. Wilson and Zoe on another. Seated in armchairs in between the sofas were Evan and Lizzie Ballard.

Emma stepped back, trying to leave as quickly as possible.

"Were you looking for someone, Mrs. Berry?" Mrs. Lockwood asked, not unkindly.

"Oh, er, Lieutenant Forrester," Emma said, wishing she could just disappear. "I thought he might be in the office. I spoke to him there yesterday."

Her mother was going to hear about this social gaffe. She could just see Mrs. Wilson storing it up to talk about later. She was sure Zoe Wilson was smirking.

"He isn't. And in any case, there is a door from the outside if you need to find him at some time."

"Thank you. Please excuse me."

Rather than traipse back through the dining room and the vestibule as if she had a right to be in the homestead anyway, Emma crept as quietly as possible out the front door, all thought of finding the Lieutenant banished from her mind. All she wanted was to get back to Deelie's cottage and hide her face. She stopped in the garden for a moment to compose herself and then went through the gate to the cottages.

Margaret, Katherine and Laura were playing skip rope on the grass in front of the schoolhouse. Emma could just see Jonathan in the shadows, absorbed in something on the trunk of the willow tree. Ann must be in the classroom. Perhaps she could have a word wih her now, while she was free. It was too good an opportunity to pass up, regardless of how she was feeling.

Jonathan jumped and put his back to the tree as she stepped on the verandah. Emma smiled to her-self. He'd been carving something in the tree trunk. The schoolroom was empty apart from the usual classroom furniture – a handful of desks, a teacher's table, blackboard, drawings pinned to the walls.

"Miss Russell? Ann, are you there?"

Emma crossed the classroom to a passage at the far end. Off the passage was a door leading into another room. She knocked on it. No answer. She turned the knob and quickly looked in. It was Ann's bedroom. Sparsely furnished but neat, with a single bed covered in a bright quilt, a small closet, and a chest of drawers on top of which was a bowl and jug for washing. A window in the far wall looked out to the willow tree.

Emma tried another door at the far end of the passage. It opened to the back yard by a small set of wooden steps. An outhouse was situated a little further down the yard. Not wanting to disturb Ann if she was in there but hoping to catch her, Emma sat down on the steps and waited.

She had barely arranged her skirts when she heard voices. Looking across she saw Ann and Ruth at Ruth's back door. As Ann turned toward the schoolhouse her foot seemed to hover for a moment at her seeing Emma sitting there.

"Am I being checked up on," she asked boldly, as she reached the corner of the schoolhouse.

"Everyone is, I'm afraid," Emma told her.

Ann bristled. "I shouldn't be in trouble for visiting with Ruth. She's extremely low right now. It's the least I can do."

"I would be the last to deny that," Emma replied.

Ann looked a little taken aback but rallied quickly. "I was just surprised to see you here."

"Mmm. I know the Lieutenant will have spoken to you, but I'm checking with everyone to see if they have remembered anything more. Can you tell me what you did when you heard the explosion?"

"I was in the classroom, of course. I just froze when I heard the noise. People were shouting. The children were frightened, so I took a quick look outside to see what was happening. Then I had to explain to them what was going on and calm them. But I couldn't just sit there if I could help, so I took the children out front with me and helped on the bucket line."

"Did you see anyone?"

Ann hesitated. "I saw Gladys. She was hanging the wash for Naomi and Harold was there talking to her. They're sweet on one another, you know." She gave Emma a sideways look. "How was your outing with Evan? I see you took Deelie along as chaperone. That was clever of you. Mother Lockwood would have approved."

"I won't hold you up any longer," Emma said ignoring Ann's comments. She had confirmed Harold's alibi. Another one down.

"Give my regards to the Lieutenant."

"Emma." Barbara accosted her from the garden. "Do you have a moment?" Emma joined her on the other side of the fence. "The Lieutenant is still away around the men, so you won't find him right now. At least you gave Ma an opening to end the Wilson visit," she said.

"Oh, lordy." Emma didn't need to be reminded of her social gaffe.

"Ma's exhausted but that woman insists on visiting and talking about herself on the pretext of offering support and sympathy." Barbara put her hand on Emma's arm. "Come sit down."

"I feel dreadful," Emma lamented, as she let Barbara lead her to the garden bench. "I embarrassed myself and your mother, walking about the place as if I owned it."

"Don't worry. It will be forgotten tomorrow."

It wouldn't of course, not by Mrs. Wilson, anyway. It could get back to Mrs. Keogh, too. She needed that woman to have a good opinion of her, at least for the moment.

"I'm more interested in what you said to Evan during your little jaunt this morning," Barbara went on. "after the way he behaved in the drawing room. He was talking to Lizzie, and Zoe was wearing herself out trying to get his attention. I thought it was Zoe he was interested in, but now I wonder if he was just being polite. He is sometimes too nice for his own good Evan, especially where women are concerned." Everyone kept saying that, but Emma hadn't especially noticed it this morning.

"And Zoe does put herself forward," Barabara said. "Lizzie, now, she has twice the brains and would make a useful wife." Especially with her useful inheritance, Emma thought. "But I digress. Have you definitely put Evan off?"

It seemed everyone had known about this matchmaking plot.

"He was never on, Barbara, I'm sorry. I'm not in the market for a husband."

"Shame. I would have liked you for a sister-in-law, but you'd be bored to tears here. I could see that the moment I met you."

"I fear I have disappointed your mother."

"She'll get over it. I'm going to push for Lizzie, anyway. Tell me what has the Lieutenant discovered? We know you are working with him, and Naomi told me you'd spoken to her and Ruth yesterday." She looked at Emma anxiously.

"Can I ask you some questions?" Emma said in response, putting herself into evidence collecting mode. She didn't want to give anything away.

"I've already spoken to Lieutenant Forrester. But go ahead. I won't promise to answer if it incriminates me." She tried to make it sound a joke, but it fell flat.

"Where were you when the mill exploded?"

"We'd finished cleaning up after breakfast and done a little baking and I'd just finished making butter. The butter churn is on the side verandah off the kitchen. I was about to go in. It was nearly time for morning tea, and everyone would be back shortly. I was turning toward the kitchen door when the explosion..." She paused and swallowed. "Things were flying through the air and Ian... he was getting to his feet and then he fell."

Emma patted her arm. "I'm sorry. What did you do?"

"I ran out. Mrs. Fowler was behind me. And then Dec was there. We were just staring at the mill. It was so quiet when everything stopped falling. Except for the flames roaring. Nothing was moving there." She shuddered.

Emma waited a moment for Barbara to compose herself. "Do you know where anyone else was before the explosion?" she asked.

"Um, Dec was in the office. He'd asked me to bring his morning tea there later. I don't know... Gladys and Holly would have gone to the cottages. Ma was in the kitchen with Mrs. Fowler, I think. Anyway, she came out at once. Everyone was just going about their normal work. I don't pay much attention to what the boys are doing day to day."

"Was Declan normally in the office?" Naomi had said it was Declan who looked after the bookwork, but it didn't hurt to get another opinion.

"Quite a lot. Andy hated the paperwork. He was always talking and planning. He had long-range ideas, as he used to call them."

"Did they include expanding Evan's vineyard and setting up a store for Harold?"

Barbara gave her a shrewd look. "You have been busy, haven't you? I knew you were smart."

"I'm surprised Andrew spent so much time working in the mill, I would have thought he'd leave that to one of his brothers, or an employee, Brendan perhaps."

Barbara looked conflicted for a moment. "Oh, it doesn't matter now, anyway," she said. "Andy was going to burn down the old mill when the new one was ready, so we'd collect the insurance. He was working there to make sure everything went right, that it was all under control." Her voice caught for a moment.

"We aren't doing anything illegal," she went on. "I mean, not now, after the way it's turned out anyway. The mill exploded by accident. There's nothing suspicious about it."

Emma nodded. She had begun to suspect something like this. "So that little fire in the mill the day or so before I arrived, would that have been an experiment? Setting the scene?" Barbara nodded. "And the next time he wouldn't put it out but let it burn." Bile rose in her throat. "Did the miller know about the risk he was taking?"

Brighten had blamed Brendan for the fire, so Andrew couldn't have told him of his plans for the mill. Defrauding the insurance wasn't news you spread about. He'd have wanted it kept within the family.

"Andy would have made sure no one was hurt."

"But he didn't. And they were, weren't they?"

"It was an accident," Barbara cried.

Emma shook her head. "Perhaps he tried another test, and it went too far. Did you all know about the plan to burn the mill for the insurance to pay for everyone's projects?" She made no apology for sounding harsh. They had literally been playing with fire and people's lives.

Barbara's face crumpled into tears. "They've been paid for in blood now, haven't they?" she sobbed. "That's why we know it wasn't one of us. We had no need. That clears any of us, don't you see? Everyone was going to get what they wanted, and Andy would still have a flour mill."

Barbara was hunting blindly in her pockets for a handkerchief. "It was an accident," she repeated. "That arrow was just lying about." She sniffed again and wiped her eyes.

Andrew had told Emma the mill was going to be used for firewood when she'd asked. She thought if anything amused him it would have been saying something like that.

Barbara balled her handkerchief in her hands. "We all know the explosion in the mill was just a terrible accident. But Frank doesn't believe it. Andy was perfect as far as he was concerned. He wouldn't make a mistake that caused the mill to explode while he was in it. That's why he says it was deliberate."

Emma remained sitting in the garden after Barbara left. She would have to talk to the Lieutenant as soon as possible. She had expected to have to ask more questions about the insurance, even put her theory forward and have it denied. But Barbara had been quick to explain and Emma didn't know why. Worse still, it didn't help Brendan.

Chapter 22

Emma Is Annoyed

AFTER A QUIET lunch at the cottage, Emma went in search of the Lieutenant and met Barbara leaving Ruth's cottage.

"The Lieutenant is back," Barbara told her. "He's in the office."

"Thank you. I'll go around then."

"Don't be silly. I'll take you there."

In the drawing room, voices could be heard through the closed office door. Barbara knocked and opened it. Emma could see Frank Lockwood in the chair she had sat in yesterday.

"Mrs. Berry is here to see you, Lieutenant."

"Thank you, Miss Lockwood. Would you ask her to wait, please?"

"Certainly." Barbara closed the door. "You heard?"

Emma nodded and chose an armchair some way from the office door. Barbara made to leave but stopped at the drawing room door.

"You're going to tell him, aren't you? About the insurance?"

"Would you prefer I didn't?"

Barbara looked a little nonplussed. It obviously wasn't the response she expected – or wanted, Emma was sure.

"Oh, whatever you think best," she managed to say. "It doesn't reflect well on us, I know, but it means none of us had a motive."

"Possibly."

Barbara hesitated a moment but left the room without saying anything more. Emma turned her attention to the office. She could hear the murmur of voices but could not make out what was being said.

It must have been all of twenty minutes before the office door opened and Lieutenant Forrester invited Emma in. She was beginning to think he had forgotten her. Frank Lockwood wasn't in the office, having apparently left by the outer door. As Emma took her seat, she wondered what he could have to say that would have taken such a time.

"What's this I hear about you going down to Evan Lockwood's vineyard?" he said without preamble, taking his seat behind the desk. "You didn't tell me you were planning on doing that."

"I didn't know about it when I was speaking to you yesterday," Emma said, wondering why talking to Evan would bother him. "I met Evan by chance, and we arranged it."

"You don't make my life any easier by putting yourself in danger. It's why the police are always reluctant to let an amateur get involved in an investigation. I should never have agreed to what you wanted. Evan Lockwood is still a prime suspect and going down there alone..."

"I wasn't alone," Emma assured him before he could go on. "Deelie came with me and Mrs. Lockwood packed us a picnic morning tea. It was hardly a dangerous situation. Everyone knew where we were."

Lieutenant Forrester didn't look any less annoyed, but it was now tinged with embarrassment. "I wasn't told that."

"Who told you what I was doing? No, let me guess." If he hadn't been given the full details, there was only one person she could think of who would set out to cause trouble. "It was Ann Russell, wasn't it?" The Lieutenant acknowledged it was. Emma thought it best to move on. "I can tell you Evan Lockwood is not romantically involved with Ruth Lockwood, although she may wish him to be. He has his eye on young Lizzie Ballard, the doctor's niece. But he does keep a bow and arrows down at the vineyard."

"Does he now?" said the Lieutenant. "Did you ask him what he uses it for?"

"Shooting the birds that attack the grape crop when it is ripening. I suggested it wasn't a very efficient method of repelling them but apparently he also uses netting."

"To catch the birds?"

"No, to cover the rows of vines. Orchardists use netting to protect their fruit trees."

"So, Evan could still have come up along the river, shot the arrow into the mill and then turned up after a suitable amount of time as if he had just come from the vineyard."

"He could." She didn't think so, but her opinion meant nothing in the scheme of things. "Ann Russell has confirmed Harold's alibi too. She saw him talking to Gladys in the backyard, as he says."

"Good," he made a note in his notebook.

"Did you learn anything useful this morning?" Before she told him what she had learnt about the mill insurance, she wanted him to share what he had been doing.

"The two men working on the brickwork for the new mill alibi one another. One of them was knocked down on the platform by the blast. Had some bruising on his arms. The other was hauling up a bucket of mortar on a pulley and almost ended up with it on his head when he lost hold of the rope."

"Goodness. It's lucky there were only two deaths. What about the station hands?"

"Several of them heard the explosion but thought it might have been thunder, given the weather. Couldn't shake them. But I can't see any motive there

either. They don't seem to have had any disagree-
ments with Andrew Lockwood and they didn't know
the miller. Nothing of any use except for
elimination."

"I have learned something of interest," Emma
said. "Though, like you, I don't think it adds much to
the problem." Lieutenant Forrester looked at her
expectantly. "According to Barbara Lockwood,
Andrew was planning to burn down the old mill, once
the new mill was up and working, and claim the
insurance. Everyone who wanted money for a project
would get their share. That means, according to
Barbara, no one in the family had a motive to blow
up the mill, or kill Andrew."

"Barbara Lockwood told you that, did she?" He
looked thoughtful. "How interesting, how very
interesting."

"You know something," Emma said. "What is it?
Have you looked at their financial situation?"

"I have looked at the financial records. And
spoken to Declan Lockwood. All their ready cash is
going into the new mill, but Andrew did have stocks
and shares bought by Xavier Lockwood. He could
have realised the funds needed readily enough from
those, but he wouldn't sell, or borrow against them."

"Does Declan feel the same way about that, or is
he planning to use them?"

"He says not. I also asked if the mill was insured.
Declan said they had a policy for accidental damage.

It was the normal policy people take out against property damage. I don't know if you are aware of what that means, Mrs. Berry. A policy for accidental property damage does not cover damage caused by a malicious act."

"Oh, my goodness. So, if we found evidence that someone had caused the mill to explode – a malicious act if ever there was – the insurance company wouldn't pay up. Do you think Declan understood that?"

"I didn't mention it but when I left him, he was looking over the policy."

Emma struggled to get her thoughts in order. "When did you speak to Declan about this?"

"Yesterday evening." Emma caught his eye and he nodded. "Time enough for them to come up with a plan to ensure the explosion is marked as an accident."

Emma rubbed her forehead. "I was concerned how readily Barbara told me about what Andrew was planning. I already had a fair idea of what was going on after I'd spoken to Mrs. Fowler. The little fire in the mill caused by a nail between the millstones – he'd set that up himself, as a test run. And he was working in the mill himself to manage things, rather than give the job to a station hand or one of his brothers."

"The evidence does tend to lean that way."

Emma nodded. "Barbara used me to deliver this information, didn't she? It looks better this way, as though it was wrangled out of them rather than they boldly offered it up to make sure they got the insurance pay out."

"The end result is the same."

"Yes, but it looks better. This way you may not even mention it in your report."

"That is true."

Emma felt suddenly tired as if she had been put through the mangle and squeezed dry by the machinations of the Lockwood family.

"But what about Frank Lockwood?" Emma asked remembering he had been speaking to the Lieutenant for some time while she waited. "What does he have to say about all this?"

"Ah yes, Frank Lockwood. The final piece in the puzzle." Emma waited. "Frank Lockwood provided an alibi for your friend O'Neill."

Emma thought she must be confusing the names of the brothers. Or the Lieutenant was.

"Who did you say confirmed Brendan's alibi?"

"Frank Lockwood."

"Frank Lockwood?"

Lieutenant Forrester looked up and around the room. "I've never noticed an echo in here before."

Emma was sure she was gaping at him. She shook her head completely bewildered. Was he smirking?

"How…?"

Lieutenant Forrester leaned back in his chair, pleased to see her at a loss, Emma was sure.

"Frank Lockwood told me he went to the stable this morning, and when he was walking back toward the barn he had this flash of memory, of seeing O'Neill running from the outhouse as the sky above the barn turned red. You remember Frank was working in the stable at the time of the explosion?"

Emma nodded. "How very convenient to have recovered that memory."

"It's not unheard of," Lieutenant Forrester said. "In my experience, questioning witnesses a second time after several days have elapsed can often reveal an extra detail or two. As if the mind has processed the matter in the meantime."

Emma realised she had said much the same when she questioned Ann a little while ago.

"So, with Brendan's alibi confirmed, and no one in the family supposedly having a motive because of the insurance money for their projects, and there being no other motives or suspects, I guess the explosion will have to be declared an accident." Emma could imagine the relief this would bring her friends. "Did Frank explain why he accused Brendan in the first place?"

"He said the miller had accused O'Neill of putting the nail between the millstones and causing the first fire to get rid of him, so Frank just thought it was another attempt on O'Neill's part."

"How very convenient. Brendan did tell me the miller accused him of that."

Lieutenant Forrester let out a heartfelt sigh. "Except Frank still believes the explosion was caused by a flaming arrow. He won't accept the arrowhead got there any other way."

They were both silent, lost in thought for a moment.

"A complete waste of time as I expected," the Lieutenant said finally closing his notebook. "I will be putting it down as an accident. The worst the Lockwoods can be accused of is planning to defraud the insurance company, and I don't see the point of mentioning it in my report as they didn't succeed. Better to keep it simple."

EMMA, DEELIE and Brendan ate supper at the Felling's cottage that evening. Everyone had heard the Lieutenant's conclusion that the explosion at the mill had been accidental. Frank apologised to Brendan for the accusations he had made against him, citing shock and grief. It was received with some doubt as to truth and motive, but no one was unhappy at the outcome. Emma had no real basis for disagreeing with the Lieutenant's conclusion, though she wished she didn't feel she had been out-manoeuvred.

She was awake early next morning with the immediate thought she had never told the Lieutenant about the gate beside the cottage. And she hadn't walked along the river from there. In fact, she had never got to walk along the river at all. She decided she would do it now to satisfy her own curiosity as to how plausible it would have been for someone to have used the gate to reach a spot below the mill site.

As soon as the sun peeped over the horizon and brightened the bedroom a little, she dressed quickly, tying her hair back with a ribbon. She slipped out without disturbing Liam.

The gate to the river opened without a squeak, but before she could step through Alfie rushed by almost tripping her. She was annoyed with herself for not checking where he was.

"Alfie. Come back here."

Alfie kept going, disappearing along the bank. Emma was afraid to raise her voice and wake anyone. She remembered the pieces of beef jerky wrapped in paper in her jacket pocket. She would entice him back with a piece, if she could find him.

Concentrating on what she had set out to do, she tried to put herself in the place of a person creeping along the river that morning. What would they have seen or heard? She and Deelie had been sitting out in front of the cottage. Anyone creeping past might have heard them talking and would have tried to be as far from them as possible so as not to be heard themselves. But on the morning of the explosion the creaking of the mill sails, and rumble of the machinery would have covered any noise. If someone had been there, they could have hurried not needing to take much care.

The water was dark, the sun not high enough yet to reach it through the trees as she made her way quickly along the curve of the bank. Something plopped into the depths as she passed. She made herself step quietly, then stopped for a moment and listened. Through the cheeping of the thornbills and chittering of the fairy wrens above her as they woke to the day, she could just hear Alfie rustling somewhere ahead. At least she hoped it was the little dog and not rats.

It was only a matter of minutes before she was below the mill site. There was the bank of the billabong, above her. She crept up. The mill would have hidden her from the front of the homestead. There was a tree large enough to stand beside to shoot, making it difficult for anyone inside the barn or the smithy to see her.

Alfie was nearby snuffling at something in a clump of grass. She took out the paper with the beef jerky wrapped in it and held out a piece.

"Here boy, Alfie. Here. See what I have for you."

He came running, tail wagging excitedly. As he ate the jerky, she pulled the ribbon from her hair and tied it to his collar to form a short lead.

"Good boy." Alfie pulled ready to run again. "Not this time," Emma told him.

She had to bend to keep hold of the ribbon. It wasn't the most comfortable way to traipse along a riverbank. Alfie kept getting side-tracked with scents, and she had to keep hauling him out of bushes and from behind tree trunks. She was relieved when they reached the gate and were safely inside the yard again. She rescued her ribbon and put her hand in her jacket pocket to give Alfie another piece of jerky when her fingers found something hard and round. She pulled it out. It was a silver boot button. She turned it over in her hand. Of course. Liam had found it in the sand-pit. She had forgotten all about it.

Boot buttons were always coming loose and getting lost. They had been the bane of her life as a child, as she tried to keep up with her older brothers, climbing trees, getting into scrapes. Her mother had finally made her sew them back on herself, hoping it would convince her to behave in a more ladylike manner. Between boot buttons and darned stockings, she had disliked needlework ever since.

The button in her hand had a few broken threads twisted around the shank. It reminded her of the arrowhead with its piece of wire and scrap of cloth. As she looked at it, she realised there was one person who actually didn't have an alibi confirmed by anyone else. And she did have a motive if what she'd heard was correct.

Was Frank right after all?

Chapter 23

One Last Play

"GOOD MORNING," Emma called, as Ann came from the schoolhouse heading for the vestibule and breakfast.

Ann looked surprised at seeing her sitting in the garden. She stepped toward the gate. Behind her, Alfie ran around with a toy soldier in his mouth.

"You're out early. Are you waiting for someone?"

"I was waiting for you. Won't you join me?"

"I was about to have breakfast."

Emma held up a basket. "I have breakfast."

"How odd. Why would I have breakfast out here with you?"

"Because I want to talk to you about Frank," Emma said, lowering her voice so that it barely carried. "Where no one can overhear us."

The woman looked at her quizzically for a moment.

"The schoolhouse would be warmer if you want privacy," she said.

"Someone may be hanging about and overhear us. There are ears everywhere." As Ann would know. "We can see anyone approaching here."

"Oh, well. I suppose."

She came through the gate, not hurrying. Alfie took the opportunity to slip through with her. He came straight for Emma and sat, looking at her expectantly. She gave him her last piece of jerky. He was learning to attend at least, if only for the jerky.

"Do sit down," Emma said, as Ann stopped in front of her. "Mrs. Fowler has packed us lovely thick slices of toast, and there's marmalade, and tea to wash it down. We even have a rug for our legs."

Ann sat, a look of condescending amusement on her face. Emma spread the rug, tucking it in around them both. The folding table in front of her was laid out with settings for two.

"This feels like a child's tea party," Ann said as Emma poured tea.

"Sugar?"

"Two lumps."

Emma obliged, putting one lump in her own cup.

"So, what is this about Frank, Mrs. Berry?" Ann asked, stirring her tea carefully.

"Please call me Emma. May I call you Ann?"

"Certainly."

"It's about the mill explosion."

Ann tapped the spoon on the edge of the cup and put it on the saucer.

"What about it?"

"You must be concerned, considering you and Frank are courting. I have heard correctly about that haven't I? The information came from Mrs. Fowler. Of course, she did say it seemed to have, let's say, lost some impetus lately."

Ann laughed. "Oh, Mrs. Fowler. Typical. Servants love to gossip and create problems where there aren't any. Their lives are so dull. I can't believe you would give credence to their nonsense. Why is our relationship of any interest to you? Or do you need some more intrigue now that the mill investigation has been finalized? Without anything lurid being uncovered, I might add. That must have been disappointing after all your questioning."

"Unfortunately, Frank still believes the explosion was caused deliberately, either to kill the miller or Andrew. The Lieutenant, as you would no doubt have heard has after a rigorous investigation declared it an accident."

"Which it was. Obviously."

"You thought that did you? Even when it was Frank who made the accusations of murder?"

"I do have a mind of my own, Mrs. Berry."

"Emma, please."

"Emma. Frank had, shall we say, an unusually strong belief in the perfection of his older brother."

"And you didn't agree with that assessment, did you?"

"I did not. Andrew Lockwood ruled this family. No one did anything without his say so. They will all be better off without him, tragic as it is."

"And Frank in particular will be better off, won't he?"

"They all will."

Emma buttered a slice of toast and opened the jar of marmalade. "Have you tried this? Oh, of course you would have. It's delicious, isn't it? Just the right sharpness."

Ann put down her cup. "This is really quite tedious. Is there anything else?"

"I'm sorry, I digress. It's just that Frank is going to be standing alone on this matter of murder and he needs a friend, someone who can offer him some consolation. That's where you come in, Ann. You can help convince him that it was an accident and give him peace of mind."

"I see. Yes, I could certainly do that. Though I don't understand why you are bothering with it."

"Well, because there's just one problem."

"Oh? And what is that?"

"I believe Frank is right. I believe someone did shoot a flaming arrow into the mill, bizarre and unbelievable as it may seem."

"How interesting I'm sure. So, do you need consoling and convincing that it was an accident, too? And why would I care?"

"I thought you might be able to clear up a few matters for myself and Frank, put our minds at rest."

"Have you spoken to Frank about this?"

"No, I have not," Emma replied, quite truthfully. She leaned toward Ann, lowering her voice. "You see, we have confirmed alibis for everyone except Evan Lockwood and yourself. Now, given the insurance plan that Andrew had concocted – you didn't know about that? Well, hardly surprising, really. It was kept strictly within the family so there is no reason why you would have been told. Even by Frank. Suffice to say that because of it, it seems that no one in the family had a credible motive for blowing up the mill, so that leaves Evan out. And we can't find any reason why they would want to get rid of the miller, either. Jack Brighten had no contact with any of the women-folk, and the only person he aggravated was Brendan O'Neill, who also has a solid alibi. From Frank him-self, no less." Emma looked to Ann. "So, what have you to say for yourself?"

Ann laughed. "You're suggesting I did it? How ridiculous. I have an alibi, remember. I was in the schoolroom. Nowhere near the mill. Of course, no one would have seen me to confirm that. You could ask the children of course, but what would they know? They can't remember half of what they are taught as it is. And what on earth possible reason could I have had anyway?"

"Well, that's what I want you to clear up for me, Ann. Has Frank asked you to marry him?"

Ann bristled. "Really, Mrs. Berry…"

"Emma."

"Emma." Her name sounded as sour as lemon on Ann's lips. "Your questions are most impertinent. Yes, he has, if you must know."

"Oh? But why hasn't it been announced? Is there something holding it back?"

"Well, clearly. The family is in mourning. It wouldn't be appropriate just now."

"That situation has existed for less than a week. What was holding up the announcement before Andrew Lockwood's death?" Emma paused for a moment. "He didn't approve of Frank marrying you, did he?"

"You're wrong. Frank and I will marry."

"Perhaps. But only because Andrew isn't here to insist on a wife bringing something to the family. And you don't have anything, do you?"

"I have my teacher training."

"But that wasn't enough for Andrew, was it? It isn't something tangible like a livery stable or a riverboat, is it? It isn't something of monetary value." Ann glared at her. "So, here's what happened as I see it. I want you to consider it carefully, so you can point out where it's wrong.

"You decided that if Andrew wouldn't approve your marriage to Frank you would have to get rid of him. You knew about flaming arrows because you were here when the family put on that display for their mother's birthday last year. And you knew about the dangers of flour dust. You read the newspapers, it was spoken about often enough, wasn't it?"

"Of course, I knew about those things. Everyone here does. But I was at the schoolhouse when the mill exploded. I told you that. And I was there on the bucket line with everyone else."

"You were on the bucket line, indeed. But you weren't in the classroom when the mill exploded. You were down behind the mill having shot an arrow in through a window."

Ann laughed. "Oh, that's rich. How did I manage to do that?"

"Well, you left the children working on their lesson with strict instructions not to leave the room. Then you slipped out across the backyard to the gate behind Deelie's cottage, along the river to the back of the mill, shot the arrow, threw the bow and anything else in the river, and ran back. You had probably hidden the things you needed down there at some time so they would be handy. It only took a matter of minutes to get back."

Emma took a sip of tea. "You expected the children might venture out eventually, to see what was happening, but you had told them to wait and they would have, for a while at least, long enough you thought, for you to get back. You may have counted on them being too frightened to venture out. Perhaps you had even locked them in. Your delay in getting to the front of the homestead at once could be excused by having to calm the children and make sure it was safe for them to come out."

"Hah. I couldn't have done that without being seen. Gladys was in the backyard, hanging out the wash and talking to Harold. I told you that."

"As you said. So, you had to go out by the gate at your end of the yard and down the outside of the fence, along the back through the bush, and back up along the river."

Ann laughed again. "You would have seen me if I'd done that."

"Would I?"

"Of course. You were sitting out with Deelie and Ruth."

"So we were. My, my, you were busy, checking on everyone's whereabouts, weren't you? It doesn't make any difference. You would have no trouble climbing over the fence. Even Alfie can do that, so I've been told, but you may have used a chair to stand on. You were hidden from Gladys and Harold, and from Deelie and me, by the schoolhouse. And there was no one else outside to see you. Evan was down at his vineyard, Frank was in the stables, Brendan in the outhouse, Declan indoors in the office. Everyone else was going about their work in the homestead and the cottages.

"It took longer going around the back of the yard, but it didn't matter how long it took on the way there. It only mattered to get back quickly, and you were able to use the gate beside Deelie's cottage then. No one was in the yard after the mill exploded. We had all run to the front. You brought the children with you when you came. If anyone noticed how long it was after the explosion before you arrived, they wouldn't have thought anything of it. Of course, you were being responsible considering the children's welfare."

"Sorry to disappoint you but none of your theories, interesting and creative as they are, mean anything," Ann said, putting her cup down carefully on the table. Emma was heartened to see her hands were not entirely steady. "I often slip out for a breath of air or to freshen up when I've set the children some work to do. I could count the minutes I'm away on the fingers of one hand. I know I said I was in the classroom when the mill exploded but I was actually in the outhouse. I was feeling a little off colour that day. I may have been away a little longer than usual. You don't imagine I wanted to discuss that with you, and I certainly wasn't about to discuss it with the Lieutenant."

"The Lieutenant will speak to the children, of course," she said. "I'm sure the older ones will be able to tell us more."

"They will confirm what I have just told you."

Emma heaved a great sigh. "Well, I guess in that case, the deaths of Andrew Lockwood and Jack Brighten will have to go down as an accident after all."

Ann's laughter trilled. "Nice try. May I go now?"

"Yes, of course. Sorry to hold you up. Oh, I think this might belong to you." Emma put out her hand with the silver boot button resting on her palm.

"Oh, I'm sure it does," Ann said promptly taking it. She poked her foot out to display the silver buttons on her black boots. "They are very smart, aren't they? Where did you find it?"

"On the other side of the schoolhouse, by the fence. Perhaps you caught it on the way over. It was nice of Ruth Lockwood to give you a packet of silver buttons, wasn't it? I doubt you could afford them on a teacher's wage. And both pair of boots, too. It must have rankled though, Ruth handing you the buttons like the lady of the mansion dispensing largesse to the lower classes. And her no more than the daughter of a convict. You hated that Andrew had accepted Ruth and Naomi into the family, even marrying Ruth himself, but refused to accept you."

Ann hissed. "They think they are so much better than me, as if I'm just a servant. Me, a schoolteacher. Just because they are Lockwoods now."

"Which you desperately wanted to be yourself so you could feel superior, but Andrew Lockwood was preventing it. And you were afraid Frank would give up eventually, weren't you, so you had to get rid of Andrew before Frank lost interest. Or was he already? How old are you Ann? Did you feel time was running out for you? Did you…"

"You think you are so smart," Ann snarled. "But I couldn't have done it, no matter what you think. I don't know how to use a bow. You didn't consider that did you, Mrs. Berry?" Her name on Ann's tongue was little more than a sneer.

"You don't know how to use a bow?" Emma said, more loudly. Ann looked quickly behind, alarm showing for an instant, but there was no one in sight. "But you told me the day Frank found the arrowhead that the men liked to teach the women how to shoot. Ian said everyone who lives here is taught. Are you saying no one taught you? Frank perhaps?"

"No, he did not. No one did."

"Yes, I did."

Ann screamed and leapt to her feet as Frank Lockwood stepped out from the trees behind them. He looked sadly at her.

"I would have wore him down, Ann. He would have given his blessing eventually. I told you to be patient."

"No, it's all lies. She can't prove anything, Frank."

"Swear to me, Ann. Swear on the lives of our future children, you didn't do this."

Ann stared at him. She opened her mouth, but no words came out.

Frank shook his head. "I even accused my own brothers," he said. "I didn't want to believe..." He turned away. Lieutenant Forrester appeared behind him.

"Ann Russell. I'm arresting you for the murder of Andrew Lockwood and Jack Brighten. Anything you say..."

"No, no. Frank, please. I did it for you. He was controlling all our lives, yours especially. Frank! Frank!" she screamed at his back as he walked away, head down, shoulders sagging. She turned to Emma, lunging at her. "Why couldn't you leave it alone? What did it matter to you? You have everything."

Emma dodged behind the bench out of the way of Ann's flailing hands. The breakfast table toppled amid a clatter of crockery as the Lieutenant restrained her.

Alfie, hoping for some fallen goodies, dashed through Emma's legs, tripping her. As she fell her left arm hit the edge of the millstone memorial. She heard the crack, the pain a red flash coursing up her arm and through her head.

Epilogue

What Now?

LIEUTENANT FORRESTER called next day. Catherine showed him into the drawing room, where Emma was sitting by the fire, her arm in a gutta percha cast and a sling to support the fractured bone.

"That was a nice piece of detective work you did, Mrs. Berry," he said when he was seated and greetings exchanged. "I spoke to the two eldest Lockwood children before I left. It was as you supposed. Ann Russell left them with work to do, saying she had to leave for a few minutes. It wasn't an unusual occurrence, as she claimed. They did try to leave the schoolroom after they heard the explosion but couldn't open the doors. When she came back, she explained it away by saying the locks must need oiling. She put a cloth around the knob, pretending it was stiff, but Jonathan said the knobs were slippery. We found traces of petroleum jelly."

"How clever. If anyone had tried the doors from the outside they would have opened without any trouble. Anyone finding them locked would have been concerned."

"Indeed. She told the children what had happened and that they must be brave, and then took them out."

"I hate to rain on Emma's parade," Catherine said, almost apologetically, "but you would have known Ann Russell didn't have an alibi if you had talked to the children in the first place."

Lieutenant Forrester bristled at the implied criticism of his investigative efforts. "I wouldn't have taken the word of an eight-year-old over an adult. Especially over the boy's own teacher."

Emma nodded. "Ann would have laughed it off and claimed she took some time to check on what had happened before going back to the classroom."

"I guess I can see that could be the case," Catherine conceded. "Do I need to worry about not believing what Theo tells me when he is old enough to talk?"

"Oh dear. You are going to have to figure that one out for yourself, I'm afraid," Emma told her, laughing. "Little children have lively imaginations if Nella's brood are anything to go by, but they do learn to tell the truth from a lie eventually. After all we did, didn't we?"

Lieutenant Forrester gave an inelegant snort, causing Catherine to glance between him and Emma with increased interest. Emma ignored the

Lieutenant's insinuation that she wasn't always entirely truthful. She hadn't lied, just been economical with what she told him. Of course, he knew now she hadn't told him about the gate beside Brendan's cottage. Admitting to that had been a little embarrassing at the time.

"Was there any evidence to show Ann had climbed over the fence?" Emma asked instead.

"There were footprints that fitted her boot size on the other side in several places, and some broken twigs. Unlucky for her to have lost that boot button there."

Emma smiled. "Oh, she didn't. Liam found it in the sandpit." The Lieutenant stared at her as if she weren't quite in her right mind. "Ann had poor selfcontrol," Emma explained, "always ready with a smart remark, a little dig. I thought it might be possible to rattle her enough."

"What if she hadn't lost a button? She could have said it wasn't hers."

"It might not have been. It didn't matter. Ann wasn't about to miss the opportunity of getting another spare. Silver boot buttons don't grow on trees out there, you know. I think they were a sort of symbol for her. They fit her idea of what her future could be as a Lockwood wife. And it was Ruth Lockwood who gave them to her. Just having someone give her a packet of silver boot buttons suggested a life of ease and wealth. Her own remarks to me suggested she was envious of the life she supposed I had.

"I also got the impression she felt she wasn't given the respect her position demanded. I think she was right about that. I saw the way she was treated and spoken to, like a servant, perhaps not even as well as that, but I suspect she wasn't well liked and that was her own fault. She seemed to enjoy causing trouble with her sly remarks. Mrs. Fowler had mentioned Ann and Frank were courting but it seemed to have cooled, which made me wonder if Andrew could have had something to do with it, given his penchant for a wife to bring something of value to the family. And the fact Frank was asking Andrew for something, and told him he would continue to ask, well, I just played on what I knew."

"Well done," Catherine said.

"Indeed, as it turned out," Lieutenant Forrester admitted. "Of course, it could have led to nothing if she hadn't broken down."

"Oh, there's a back-handed compliment if ever I heard one. Damned with faint praise."

"She almost got away with it," Catherine said. "Have you found out anything about her? What might be in her background that would cause to behave in that way?"

"There hasn't been time for that. I'll be leaving it to the prosecutor in any case."

"So, what happens now?"

"I've been instructed to deliver Russell to Albury, where an officer from Sydney will meet us and take her back by train."

To a fate Emma didn't care to think about, noticing also that Ann was just Russell now.

"Have you been able to contact any of the miller's family?" she asked.

"An elderly aunt in Sussex is the only person that could be found. Always knew he would come to a bad end, was what she said."

"How sad. No one to grieve for him," Catherine said. "Unlike Andrew Lockwood."

"They might be grieving for missing out on the insurance money for the mill, too," Emma said. "I don't imagine I would be a welcome visitor there any time soon."

"Seems fitting. They were planning to get it by fraud," Catherine said.

The Lieutenant stood to leave, claiming a pile of paperwork waiting for his attention.

"I should be back at Wirramilla sometime next week, Lieutenant," Emma said. "You are welcome to call in on your way home after delivering Ann to Albury." She saw Catherine's eyebrows go up at that. "I'm going to be confined to quarters for quite some time, I'm afraid."

"Thank you. I will try and take you up on that invitation. Until then, take care of yourself and don't get into any more trouble." The cheek of the man.

"Don't get up," Catherine said to Emma. "I'll see the Lieutenant out."

"Thank you for calling," Emma told him.

"Now that is a handsome man, Emma," Catherine said when she came back into the room. "I noticed you were keen to have him call in at Wirramilla. What would Daniel say about that?"

"Oh, for... Don't you start. I hear enough of that from Lucy. What is it with everyone? Daniel doesn't care."

"I'm not so sure about that," Catherine said with a laugh. "Why else would he have you on the *Mary B*? It isn't exactly a place for a woman, even if you are his sister-in-law."

Emma didn't bother explaining it was purely a matter of economics. On his part, anyway.

When Daniel finally arrived a few days later, she hoped he might have been at least a little pleased to see her, but apparently not.

"What have you done to yourself, now?" he asked, frustration at her condition evident.

"I was tripped up by a dog, Daniel. It could have happened to anyone."

"Well, you're not going to be much use like this," he informed her. "I'll have to leave you at Wirramilla and see how we get on."

How they got on? If Daniel found they could get on well without her she may not be welcome back on the *Mary B* again, regardless of the economic benefit she was supposed to be providing.

She was glad to be back home at Wirramilla though. As she expected, her mother tut, tutted to see her in her injured state. She didn't come out and say, 'this is what you get when you mix with the lower classes,' but the implication was clear.

"I'm not going to be much help in the stillroom," Emma told her grandmother, feeling as if she were echoing Daniel.

Eleanor laughed. "Oh, you'll do," she said. "You only need one hand to stir."

Which is what she did when it was needed, as well as pull weeds in the herb garden, though she felt guilty that she wasn't of more help. Her grandmother wasn't getting any younger and the work in the stillroom was constant.

Lucy made chicken soup for her some days. Emma knew better than to tell her chicken soup was for invalids. She made if for anyone who was out of sorts in any way. A fractured arm was no different in her estimation. Emma enjoyed the soup for its warming, comforting qualities and wondered if Lucy was right. It did make her feel better when she was eating it.

She wore woollen shawls to cover her injured arm because she couldn't put it in a sleeve. Someone had to help her dress and undress. That lot usually fell to Janey, who was matter of fact, while Emma's mother, as expected, fussed too much.

Emma received several letters from Deelie written for her by Janet, except for the last one which Brendan wrote. They were doing well, Emma was pleased to hear. She hoped to see them again sometime, but not at River Bend. She didn't think the Lockwoods would care to see her either. Lieutenant Forrester hadn't visited. Perhaps he had forgotten the invitation or had been too busy. Emma had to admit to feeling a little slighted.

Six weeks after Emma came home, Nella gave birth to her fourth child. It was a girl. The delighted parents named her Daisy.

"How are you doing?" Nella asked one day, during one of Emma's many visits.

She was resting on the sofa having just fed the baby. Emma, sitting in the armchair beside her, turned from admiring Daisy in her basket to answer.

"I feel at a loose end. As if something is missing. I should be on the *Mary B,* of course. That's probably it."

"The cast should be off soon, shouldn't it? Once your arm is strong again, you'll be back on the river."

"If Daniel will allow me."

"Are you afraid he won't? Has he said something?"

"It was more like he didn't care that I wasn't able to be onboard."

"He's not a man who shows his feelings, is he."

"He shows it all right, Nell. Grumpy and complaining. At me anyway."

"From what I've seen, men often hide their softer feelings under a grumpy exterior. They're afraid they would look weak, I think. Or it embarrasses them."

Emma recalled crew member Fred Croaker's words almost a year ago, about a man not always knowing what he's feeling. He was referring to Daniel at the time. She had a fair idea what Daniel felt about her, and it wasn't comforting.

He had been helpful and supportive in delivering the Zeller children to their aunt and uncle at Kerang, during the last journey of the season back in January, and she had felt they were coming to a better understanding and acceptance of one another.

But he didn't seem to have forgiven her for the seven-and-one-half percent ownership of the *Mary B* she had given boat builder George Knowles. She had done it to get the *Mary B* back on the river, as much for Daniel's sake as for her own. So she believed anyway. Had there been, somewhere in the back of her mind, without acknowledging it to herself, the idea of keeping herself in Daniel's company?

"You do have feelings for him, don't you?" Nella said, startling her as if reading her mind.

"Don't do that," Emma told her. Nella laughed. "But is it because he's Sam's brother and reminds me of him?"

"You knew Daniel and liked him before you met Sam. He was engaged to marry someone else, wasn't he?"

"He was. She broke it off because he was away on the river so much." She hadn't given enough credit at the time to what he was going through. "She wanted a husband who was home every night."

"Well, I can't argue with that," Nella said. "But was Sam a substitute for Daniel because he wasn't available?"

"They were very different, Nell."

"Ah, but did you know that at the time? Most people are on their best behaviour while they're courting. You only learn what they're really like once you've lived with them. I suspect there was a lot to learn about Sam Berry."

Emma sighed. She couldn't disagree with that. She had been attracted to Sam's fun-loving, carefree view of life but had later discovered the irresponsible side. He had never really grown up.

Emma turned back to look at Daisy. The little girl had her father's fair colouring. She opened her eyes. She was three weeks old now, and her eye colour was just settling in. They were green, a lovely emerald green, exactly like Emma's and her grandmother's. She was certainly a Haythorne.

Emma frowned. That couldn't be right. Green eyes were in her grandmother's line, not her grandfather's. So how did Daisy end up with them? Emma's grandfather was Nella's father. Wasn't he? So how...? Oh, my.

She looked around and found Nella watching her. Emma suddenly understood the hostility that had come out on several odd occasions in the past. It was there on Nella's face now, challenging. How had Nella felt being the older daughter but never acknowledged as such? Seeing Emma reap all the benefits of the position?

Emma swallowed a lump in her throat. "We've always been more like sisters, haven't we? How long have you known?" She saw Nella's face relax.

"Grandmama told us when I was going to marry Jeff."

Emma had never heard Nella refer to Eleanor as Grandmama before. She had always said 'your grandmother' when speaking of her to Emma. It gladdened her heart that Nella could now claim the relationship openly in her presence. It was also a little unsettling. How did her father feel about Nella?

"Mother would never have let you and Lucy stay if she had known, would she?"

"That's why Grandmama talked Grandpa into taking the blame."

Did her mother suspect? It wouldn't surprise Emma if she did and would explain a lot. She resolved to be nicer to her mother in future.

When Emma's cast finally came off, she expected it to be a relief, which it was of sorts, but her muscles were stiff, and the skin on her arm was dry and scaly. Her grandmother gave her a lotion containing

calendula to use on her skin for its healing and soothing properties, and she gradually got her muscles
working, and movement back.

It was just in time. July brought a happy event with
the wedding of Matty Macdonald and Dotty Keogh
at the Keogh residence. Emma travelled to
Wentworth again, this time on the *Mary B* with Daniel
as her escort at the wedding. They joined Joe and
Catherine, the Macdonalds and the extended Keogh
family and their friends. It was a day Emma knew she
would treasure for a long time. Everyone was happy
and carefree, including Daniel, which just reminded
her how much she wanted to be back with him on the
river.

The troubles and misunderstandings of the past
had been resolved. Bea had finally forgiven Emma for
keeping secret that promise with Matty. With Dotty
about to be installed at Nettifield, she was finally able
to announce her own forthcoming marriage to
Thomas Quilp.

If only Daniel would forgive her for George
Knowles' seven-and-a-half-percent ownership of the
Mary B, the day would have been perfect. As it was,
he delivered her back to Wirramilla without a word
on when she would again be part of the crew. She
found herself reluctant to raise the matter with him.
What if he said no?

Bea visited several weeks later. "Thomas has taken
land at Wentworth, on the river almost directly across

from the wharf," she informed Emma. "He has his heart set on a vineyard." Vineyards seemed to be the coming thing.

"That will take some time to get established, though, won't it."

Bea nodded. "He will get work locally in the meantime. We'll be getting married as soon as the house is ready."

"Has your father got used to the idea of losing you as his housekeeper?" Emma asked.

"He's resigned to it," Bea said laughing. "Dotty is already taking over. She's very capable. Dad says she scares him, but that's not a bad thing. She ignores his grumbles and goes happily about doing things her own way. I don't think Matty's realised what he's let himself in for yet but it's obvious he adores her."

Everyone seemed to be moving on with their lives. Emma had a feeling of being left behind. Even her marriage to Sam seemed like it had happened to someone else. She walked along the river each day, as she had always done. There was a timelessness to the place. The river, the trees, the birds. They were always there, had always been there, unchanging. She felt she was being absorbed into the timelessness. Floss always accompanied her. Along with the occasional willy wagtail.

She realised she was beginning to feel like herself again, recovering from the loss of Sam, of the child, all she had been through in the previous year and a half. A new more confident self. There would be some who thought she was already far too confident, Daniel included.

It was a cool, cloudy day late in August when the *Mary B* called in mid-morning. It would be spring in a few days but today it was still winter. Emma and Lucy went down to the landing below the plateau to meet the boat. The crew ambled out, jackets on against the chill. Lucy urged them up to the kitchen, warm and smelling of fresh baking. They didn't need much urging. Fred winked at her as he went by.

Daniel stood on the deck and watched them go. Tall and straight, his beard neatly trimmed, brown eyes observant as he looked across at her.

"Aren't you coming up?" she asked, disappointment a lump inside her.

"I have tea on, if you'd like to come aboard."

Ah, this was it. Was she staying or was she going? She went up the boarding plank. Daniel put out his hand and helped her step onto the deck. His hand was warm in hers. She remembered Andrew Lockwood helping her up the ladder in the mill, grasping her arm. It felt nothing like that.

"Thank you," she said taking back her hand and immediately missing the warmth of his touch.

"How is your arm?"

"Almost as good as new. It aches occasionally. As if in memory." Perhaps that was what he was waiting for – a report on her health.

He led the way to the saloon on the upper level. It was pleasant, warmed from the boiler in the stokehold. The lights were lit dispelling the gloom of the day. The table was set out for morning tea, the teapot with its red padded cover, and scones with jam and cream, the jam probably Lucy's.

Emma wanted to sit and just look at the polished honey-coloured timber that lined the lower half of the walls of the saloon, the colourful posters hung above, the credenza where she kept the registers, the candelabra they used sometimes at dinner. She remembered the warmth of the crew's company and all they had been through together.

Daniel sat across from her and poured tea. Emma added sugar and milk to her cup.

"Ah Lo made you scones," he said sliding the plate toward her. "Your English lady tea as he calls it." Emma smiled. She remembered the first time Ah Lo had done that. He cleared his throat. "I've bought a house in Echuca," he said, "overlooking the river."

"Oh. That's nice."

"I spent the off-season doing it up. It was a bit rundown when I bought it, but it was a good buy. It's never flooded there, according to the neighbours."

"I see. Are you going to let it out during the season?"

"Let it? No, I don't imagine we would want to do that."

We. There was a 'we.' Of course, there would be. She stared out the window. The sky was full of grey clouds, which had suddenly become difficult to see clearly. Whoever it was would be taking her place on the *Mary B* no doubt. They would want to spend as much time as possible together. Before the children made it difficult to travel. This English lady tea of Ah Lo's, obviously ordered by Daniel, was meant to soften the blow. Ah Lo would be making it for someone else now.

"It has three bedrooms, and a porch at the front where you can sit and look out over the river. And I've started a vegetable garden. Didn't know I knew much about gardening, but it's coming on all right. Ah Lo helped me set it up, and his partner in their market garden keeps an eye on it when I'm away. I hope you like it."

She could see her future clearly now. She would be the spinster daughter at Wirramilla, taking over the making of herbal remedies from her grandmother. Joe didn't want the place, so Jeff Brackett would take on the management when her father could no longer work. He and Nella would move into the homestead eventually. She might end up living with Joe and…

"What did you say?"

"The house. I hope you like it." Emma stared. "I remember you making some comment about an armchair in your room at the Pickles boarding house. Henrietta Pickles helped me with the decorating."

"Henrietta Pickles – of the Primrose Tearoom?" Was she hearing correctly?

"She and her daughter live next door." Janet Pickles. She'd liked Janet.

"Emma, I'm asking you to marry me." Daniel hesitated as she continued to stare. She wanted to speak but her mouth didn't seem to work. He reached for her hand. "You will, won't you?" He seemed a nxious now.

Sunlight struck the corner of a cloud and sent a shaft across the saloon table, glinting off the silver sugar bowl. She realised she was smiling.

"Is that a yes?"

She nodded and he smiled. She could already hear Lucy's smug, 'I tell you.'

* * *

Next in Series

Death in Disguise

THIS ISN'T THE END. Meet Emma and Daniel again in 1884 in *Death in Disguise*. Emma, with young son Darcy, is now living in the township of Echuca in an idyllic setting on the banks of the Murray while Daniel continues to work the river on the PS *Mary B*.

But Emma is having trouble settling into town life. So, when her friend Henrietta Pickles begs her to investigate the death of her father-in-law, Emma agrees. After all, when both the Coroner and Sergeant Donovan believe Henrietta's daughter Janet is the only suspect, what else can she do?

But what are her chances of success? She's well known and respected among the rivermen, but that's hardly the best recommendation for facing down the town authorities or being accepted by the Ladies Benevolent Society. Can she do it? Find out in *Death in Disguise*.

About the Author

Irene Sauman writes historical cozy mysteries. Under her pen name, Rennae Todd, she writes cozy mysteries in a present-day setting.

Irene is a retired historian who grew up on a vineyard and orange orchard by the Murray River in New South Wales. She was an avid reader and started writing stories when she was nine years old (including some quite dreadful poetry).

Now living in Western Australia, she has three children and four grandchildren, and a sister who beta reads her books for plot holes and to see how quickly she can solve the mystery.

When not writing (or reading), Irene watches tennis, plays croquet, and has a reasonably green thumb, which means very little dies in her garden, unlike in her cozy mysteries.

Irene and Rennae share a website where you can learn more about their books, which are available in digital and print.

https://irenesaumanauthor.com

Follow us on BookBub to be notified of a new release.

https://www.bookbub.com/authors/irene-sauman

https://www.bookbub.com/authors/rennae-todd